11-13-97

To Ed D

MW01249205

Thank you for bringing
back memories of the past.

Ed Suman Jr

Signed 11-13-97 in San Diego Cal.

Sea Stories
of a
Wily Sailor

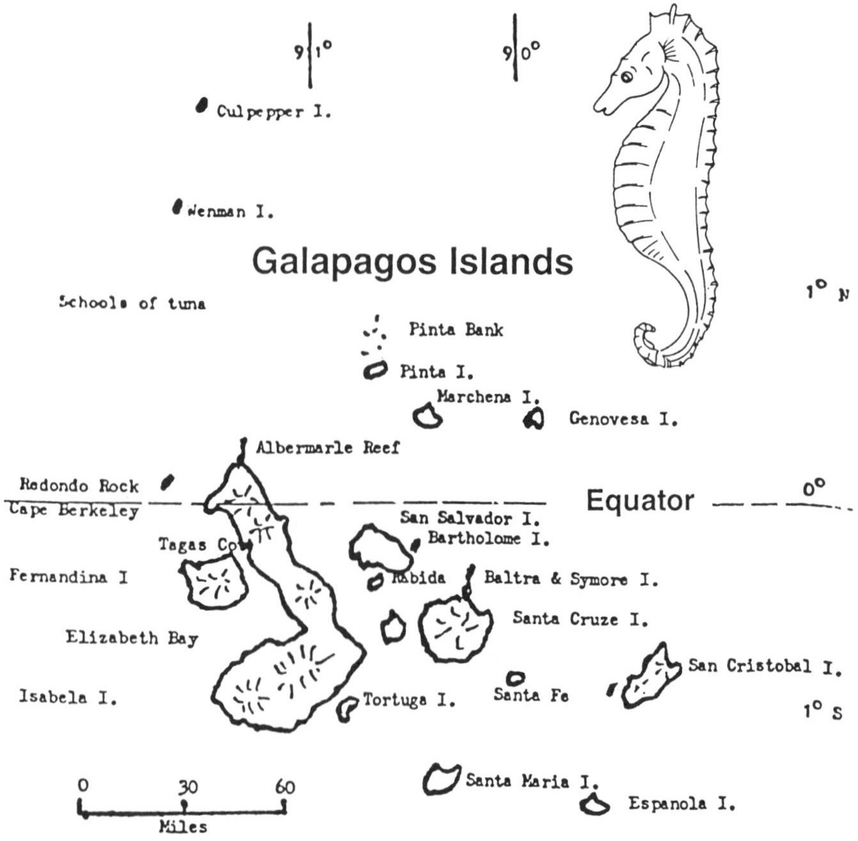
91°
90°
Culpepper I.
Wenman I.
Galapagos Islands
Schools of tuna
1° N
Pinta Bank
Pinta I.
Marchena I.
Genovesa I.
Albermarle Reef
Redondo Rock
Cape Berkeley
Equator
0°
San Salvador I.
Bartholome I.
Tagas Co
Fernandina I
Rabida
Baltra & Symore I.
Santa Cruze I.
Elizabeth Bay
San Cristobal I.
Isabela I.
Tortuga I.
Santa Fe
1° S
0
30
60
Miles
Santa Maria I.
Espanola I.

Schools of very large tuna in this area.

The Absolutely True

Sea Stories

of a

Wily Sailor

Edwin E. Suman, Jr.
La Jolla, CA

Published by Sea Stories Publications
P.O. Box 664
La Jolla, CA 92038

ISBN 0-9652537-0-8

Designed and produced by Windsor Associates,
San Diego, CA 92108
Printed in the United States of America

Dedication

To my son, Don, who would rather be a fireman.
To my daughter, Cindy, who would rather be a housewife.
To my wife, Marge, who is for eternity.

Preface

This fishing chronology is intended as a small window, where one may look into the life of a tuna fisherman. This time frame is after WWII, from 1946 to 1950. Each anecdote is true, and not intended to be a long story. These were the wild years. Most of the men that worked on the old pole boats were returning veterans of the "Big One." The attitude of these men was about the same as it had been two years before, when they were in the service of their country. They still retained that "devil-may-care" attitude.

Most of the men were single, in their twenties and thirties. A tuna boat was outfitted for three months at sea, and some of the trips were longer. I was out on the Gem of the Sea for one hundred and thirty-five days, on one trip. A very fast trip would take only sixty or seventy days.

In those years Puntarenas, Costa Rica, was a second home to many of the men. There was no law prohibiting the women from going aboard the tuna boats, and many of the men had girl friends living there. In about 1948 the government stopped the women from going aboard the tuna boats.

Because of the time spent at sea, most of the single men could not spend their hard earned money. As an example, I was ashore nine days one year and eleven days the following year. I came into San Diego on the Chicken of the Sea, carried my gear across the dock at Van Camp Cannery, and sailed on the Corsair. I made two ninety day trips to Galapagos without going ashore in San Diego.

The physical danger was ever present. We paid a fifty-cent death benefit to the union, and as I remember, one year we paid twenty-four benefits. That equates to one man dying about every two weeks! The insurance premium for a tuna fisherman was only exceeded by that of a coal miner.

Along the coast of North America, live bait was obtained utilizing a net, in the customary way. At Galapagos Islands a net was used that looked like the drapes in a house, only a lot larger. To close the net, two divers descended to the ocean floor and drug, carried, or lifted the lead line over the lava heads or other obstructions.

These divers had a hand pounded, copper helmet placed over their head and air pumped down to them, utilizing a double action hand operated pump. The helmet weighed seventy-five pounds and there was one small face plate to look out of.

Looking back over my life, I have chuckled, now and then, over various episodes that transpired. I have long thought that my children looked upon their father as something that paid the bills and made them wash the dishes. Dad was the old scoutmaster taking the Boy Scouts out on a weekend and eating their burnt offerings to the Gods - Dutch oven biscuits. Dad was the one that stood by the campfire, pointed out the various constellations in the sky and named all of the twinkling stars.

Today my children have their own homes and their own problems. Most all of the men I dealt with forty and fifty years ago are in that great world beyond.

There was a period in my life, from 1950 to 1956 approximately, when I worked on the Atlantic Reefer, Maria Inez and several others. These were small vessels that ran to South America. We hauled a little general cargo south bound, but the money was in hauling bananas north bound. We ran around both ends of Cuba, and Mr. Castro kept a weather eye on us. Every so often, we were buzzed by his fighter planes. Sometimes with our general cargo south bound, the crew would take their own "cargo." This would consist of cigarettes, whiskey, women's under clothing and handkerchiefs. We also carried cases of apples, small row boats, outboard motors and many other items.

Now and then I think of Sir Winston Churchill when he said, "There are men in the world who derive as stern an exaltation from the proximity of disaster and ruin, as others from success." There were times at sea when gale force winds laid the ocean swells down flat and white foam was all we could see. There were days and nights when I was on the bridge, with other men, just trying to keep steerage way on the ship. The times in the dead of night when you woke up to someone yelling, "Fire in the engine room! Fire! Fire!" I don't think our children will ever understand this type of life.

I looked back over my life and decided there were a lot of good stories my children should know. My wife, of forty-three years, knows many of the stories, because she lived them with me. So I am placing these recollections in print.

"Many a man puts whip and spur to his brain, but forgets too bridal his tongue." I am afraid I fall into this class. But, as Omar Khayyam said,

> "The Moving Finger writes; and, having writ,
> Moves on; nor all your Piety nor Wit
> Shall lure it back to cancel half a line,
> Nor all your Tears wash out a Word of it."

As my time is running out, I will try to put down some of my recollections, "...forgive me Lord the seas of ink I splatter, my other sins don't matter."

Edwin E. Suman Jr.

John Princiapto, I wish to thank you for your many great pictures in this little book. These are pictures that very few people will ever see, and none but us will understand.

Ed.........

Contents

BOOK I

Page	1	Bob Rood and the Shark.
Page	4	Jerry and the Alligator.
Page	5	Richard and the Big Fish.
Page	7	A Crust on a Pumpkin Pie.
Page	10	Henry and the "Old Broadbill."
Page	12	Dick Latimer Jumps Overboard.
Page	15	Harold Hits the Giant Manta.
Page	18	Who Decorated the Pelicans?
Page	21	A Dive at Rabida Island.
Page	25	Shootout at Tiger Island.
Page	28	Stay Inside or Get Shot.
Page	30	Collision At Sea.
Page	35	False Teeth in the Pie.
Page	38	Adrift at Sea.
Page	41	Big Fish on the Lawn.
Page	46	Pappy and the Deer.
Page	50	A Dive at Galapagos.

BOOK II

Page	62	The Great Anchor Drop.
Page	65	Revolution in Ecuador.
Page	69	Over the Side With Him.
Page	72	Aground in the Jambeli River.
Page	77	Building a New Rudder.
Page	81	A Trip Over the Andes.
Page	87	Fat Rosa.
Page	91	Mexican Gold.
Page	98	The Slow-Rising Yeast.

BOOK III

Page 103a   The Great Handkerchief Drop.

Page 107   A Bad Trip to Esmeraldas, Ecuador.

Page 111   The Case of Old Hook-Nose.

Page 114   Sink the Louisa.

Page 120   Illicit Cargo.

Page 132   Hot Cargo.

Page 140   Bolts of Silk.

Page 143   Fred David.

Page 150   Cut Off His Ears.

BOOK I

Fishing Boats

Bob Rood and the Shark

In La Jolla, California there is a group of exceptionally fine divers called the "Bottom Scratchers." This club is made up of men and one woman who are completely fearless, afraid of nothing in the water. One of the many requirements to enter this club is to swim out in the ocean and grab a shark, longer than you were tall, and bring it in, placing it high and dry on the beach. Bob Rood was the president of this club for seven years, and was one of those fearless few.

Bob fished on one of the old "pole boats," the ones that used live bait. Actually, Bob was with John Taso on the White Star. Bob and John met when they went to San Diego High School. This was in the days when the fishermen stood over the side of the boats in steel racks and the yellowfin tuna were caught one by one. On this trip they were fishing off Mexico, in the Revillagigedo Islands. This group of islands is located about 360 miles due west of Manzanillo, Mexico and about 200 miles south of Cape San Lucas. This group comprises San Benedicto, Socorro, Roca Partida and, 25 miles on west, Clarion.

On this clear day the seas were calm and drenched in sunlight. The White Star was drifting just off Socorro and the fish wouldn't bite. There were 300- and 400-pound tuna slowly coming up and blowing little bubbles at the live bait, then sounding into the dark depths. Bob was aggravated! Bob watched these old monstrous gran'daddies come up out of the clear blue water, blow their bubbles and then sound. The fishermen took out a harpoon and tried to hit one. That didn't work. Finally, Bob brought out his big bore rifle.

If you shoot a tuna just above his eye, he is dead instantly. Tuna are heaver than water, so they will slowly sink. Bob took his rifle, swim fins and a hay hook up on top of the canopy that covers the bait tank. He watched the giant tuna come up and go down. Finally one old gran'daddy broke the water, and Bob fired. The tuna was hit just above the eye, was dead instantaneously, and started to sink down.

Bob grabbed his hay hook, held his face mask and jumped overboard. He swam the 40 feet out to the sinking tuna and dove down. In a few seconds Bob was back up, towing a 250-pound tuna. Bob pulled for the White Star, the blood streaming out of the tuna, and the crew cheering him on. Then the dorsal fin of a big hammerhead shark started up the trail of blood. This big island shark was looking for dinner . . . but who?

The crew, cheering Bob on, now turned to yelling and pointing. When about twenty feet off the boat, Bob realized he could never outswim the shark, so he stopped dead in the water. The big shark slowly followed up the stream of blood and Bob turned and watched him, still holding the giant tuna. One of the crew picked up Bob's rifle, but John yelled at him not to shoot; the shark was to close to Bob. What happened next the entire crew watched, even the cook.

Sharks are almost blind, but they make up for this with a fantastic sense of smell. This shark was following up the blood scent, looking for a king-sized bite out of something. When the shark was about ten feet from Bob, he let the tuna go and, backing away from the blood, floated motionless in the water.

Bob very slowly extended his right arm, with his hand turned up. The huge shark was confused when he came out of the blood stream and approached Bob. The shark moved up and touched Bob's outstretched hand, pushing him to one side. As the confused shark went past, Bob dove and took hold of the tuna.

When a shark breaks out of the blood stream and is confused, he will normally sound and circle back to find the blood again. This gave Bob time to tow the old gran'daddy to the White Star. Bob pulled his prize to the ship and the crew pulled it aboard. That tuna was just a little more than 250 pounds.

There are few seafaring men that could or would be that cool in the face of a big shark, with a lot of blood in the water. It is true, there is nothing in the water that Bob Rood feared, and there is a full crew on the White Star who swear this is true.

This true story was told many times over in La Jolla, the one about Bob Rood and the shark.

Jerry and the Alligator

When there are heavy rains in Central America and the rivers are overflowing, the water becomes very muddy, and this muddy water is carried out to sea. Along with the muddy water there are other various and assorted items that go to sea, also, such as logs, dead trees, dead animals, and even live animals.

The old tuna boats, called bait boats, would go to Central America to find yellowfin tuna. First, they had to go into shallow water along the coastline to find the live bait. After finding the live bait, they would have to catch it, which entailed setting a net around the school of bait and then closing the net. Of course, what you wrapped is what you caught — not only live bait, but also logs, trees, and sometimes even snakes. When you wrapped a log, someone had to jump in the water, swim over, and roll the log over the cork line so it was clear of the net.

On this particular dark and rainy day, as we pulled in the net we found we had wrapped another log. With a sigh, Jerry said, "I'll get it," and with that, he dove over the side. This log was about thirty feet from the skiff, so Jerry started swimming. When Jerry was about four feet from the `log', lo and behold, it lifted up its long head and opened its eyes. Jerry looked at the alligator eye to eye, and both were terrified.

The alligator turned and thrashed in the net, tearing a large hole in it, while Jerry showed us his true freestyle Olympic swimming form as he swam toward the boat. If Jerry had shown this swimming form in the Olympics, no doubt we would have a new Tarzan in the motion picture industry. But, this was just another calm and peaceable day in the world of tuna fishing. So, after a quick shot of booze — for medical purposes, of course — Jerry was soon back pulling in the net.

Oh yes, the alligator; well, he wasn't a really big one. He probably ran about eight or ten feet long. Jerry told us his mouth alone was fifty feet long. And the last we saw of the alligator, he was swimming madly for the open ocean.

Richard and the Big Fish

On the old tuna boats, or bait boats as they were called in those days, we first navigated the ship to Central America, then find the live bait somewhere on the coast of Panama, Costa Rica or wherever. There was live bait to be found in the Galapagos Islands, too, but not in very great quantities. Our first choice was live bait from the coast.

On this trip we took the M.V. Corsair south to Panama. It rains almost every day in Panama, and so the rivers running into the ocean are very muddy. This mud makes the ocean water along the coast dark and muddy, also. We had cleared Panama and now had our bait permit, so we were off looking for live bait.

Our first stop was ashore to steal, or "appropriate," some pineapples, and then out to the muddy shoreline looking for live bait. We put the work boat, the big skiff, and the little skiff in the water and started along the shoreline to see what we could find. We finally saw the little telltale ripples that signaled a school of live bait, and as we went up the right-hand side, we let go the net. We turned to the left, circled the school, and picked up the little skiff, completing the set.

To move the bait from the shallow water out to the mother ship, there is an item called a "receiver," which is really nothing more than a big box with a bow. This box is about six feet wide by twelve feet long and five feet deep.

The receiver is built with a tailgate just like a pickup truck. With the receiver submerged in position, the tailgate is lowered, the net is pulled over the gate and the live bait is dumped into the receiver. Now everything is towed out to the mother ship and the receiver is made fast alongside the mother ship. The live bait is now brailed into tanks on the mother ship. Some bait boats hold 12,000 scoops of bait.

Now we had the receiver made fast to the port side of the tuna boat and we were brailing out the live bait. In short time, most of the bait was out, except for the bait that was hiding in the muddy water on the far side. At that time some tall man would usually jump into the muddy water and stomp his feet on the tin bottom, scaring the bait so they could be caught.

On this trip Richard, the brother of the Captain, a very fine young man about 6 foot 3 inches tall, was making his first fishing trip. Naturally, he was the one who jumped into the receiver. After Richard had been there a few minutes he said, "Say, there's a big fish in here."

We all laughed and told him we would show him a big fish when we arrived at Galapagos Islands.

After a few more minutes, Richard told us again, "There is a really big fish in here. I'm standing on it!" Again we laughed.

When the receiver was empty of live bait, we had to dump out the water. From the ship's deck winch and boom system, a hook was lowered into the water, then a man attached the hook to the pad eye fastened on the bow of the receiver. As the deck winch ground away, the bow of the receiver would come up, dumping out the water. On this trip, I was the man in the water who hooked up the bow, then swam to the stern and lowered the tailgate.

Everything was going along fine until the crew started to yell, and I looked up into the receiver. What I saw next was amazing! As the crew yelled for me to get clear of the receiver and out of the water, I looked up. Wedged in the receiver was Richard's "big fish", a small manta ray. The front of the manta was pushed into the bow of the receiver and the wings were curled up the sides. This manta had a wing span of about ten feet and completely covered the bottom of the receiver. How this manta ever swam past the two men at the tailgate and into the receiver is beyond imagination. Richard was right. He was standing on a big fish.

In the days that followed, we ran south to Malpelo Island, which is just a big rock sticking out of the water. Here we picked up about 40 tons of yellowfin tuna, then went on to Galapagos. On our way to Galapagos we would sit on deck in the big skiff, eating fresh pineapple and lobster tail. Along with this we'd sip a glass of red wine and retold the story of the day Richard walked on the big fish.

A Crust on a Pumpkin Pie

As I remember, it was in 1946, when we started on a long trip with the tuna boat, American Beauty. We stopped at Cedros Island and caught 200 scoops of sardines, then went around Cape San Lucas and up to Tiburon Island, then over to the east side of Baja, California, and south to Conception Bay. Going down to the end of the bay, we caught about 600 scoops of herring — Flat Iron, as the fishermen call them.

Finding no yellowfin tuna here, we headed south to Mexico and on down to the Gulf of Fonseca. We were shot at when we were in the gulf of Fonseca and returned the compliment. We ran on south to the Gulf of Nicoya and anchored at Puntarenas, Costa Rica.

By this time we were out three weeks, with no fish, we had been shot at and we were in a foul mood. We all went ashore, and a great time was had in the Union Bar. Looking back at the money spent in that bar, we should have just bought the bar.

Now it so happened that one of the engineers had a brother-in-law that he thoroughly despised. For years he and the brother-in-law would yell and argue with each other. So this engineer formed a plan. This plan was a sneaky, lowdown, rotten trick. The engineer spent a year cultivating the friendship of his brother-in-law.

Then one eventful day, we needed a cook, so the engineer told the captain he knew just the man for the job. Good cook, a real chef, lots of experience — he could really handle the job. The captain said to bring this culinary artist to the ship. The captain signed the brother-in-law on as one of the crew, and the dastardly deed was done.

This man, whom we will now call Cookie, had never cooked in his life. He was not a cook, much less a ship's cook, but the engineer had told Cookie there was nothing to being a ship's cook. All you had to do was boil a few fish heads, dish up some beans and this would be for breakfast, supper and dinner.

We all tried to help Cookie and explained that we ate very well when at sea. There is nothing much else than food to look forward to when you are at sea for weeks on end. Our trips usually ran about three months, and at one time I have been out for 135 days. Cookie worked along, but he was way out of his class. He finally learned to cook breakfast and a little more, but that was all.

Then one bright, sunny day Cookie tried his hand at baking pumpkin pies. He baked six pies and placed them on the galley table. Our smiling crew of fisherman filed into the galley to admire the handiwork of our Cookie. With looks of astonishment and in utter silence, we leered at the pumpkin pies. What met our gaze were six pumpkin pies, and each one had a crust!

We were now anchored off Puntarenas, Costa Rica, and had a night ashore. We were all up early and, with coffee in hand, we leaned on the ship's rail to listen. There were several work boats gathered around our bow, and our captain was talking with another captain in a work boat. The captains talked a lot, waving their arms, and we gathered around closer.

From the conversation, we understood that two of the crewmen on the other ship had been in a fight while ashore, and when they returned to their ship they carried on the fight. At last, one man had pulled out a long knife and killed the other. The crew had tossed the dead man overboard for the sharks. This is what the discussion had been about between the captains.

We could hear the captains talking, and we were all talking at once about the knife fight and feeding the sharks when Cookie walked up. We explained to him about the knife fight and feeding the sharks.

When Cookie asked who had been killed, we told him it was their ship's cook. When he asked why they had killed him, the redhead in our crew smiled and answered, "He put a crust on a pumpkin pie!"

The color slowly drained out of Cookie's face until he was chalk white. He turned and ran into the bunk room. We all had another sip of coffee. The next time, which was the last time, I saw Cookie, he was in the work boat with his suitcase, trying to get

8

ashore.

The captain and the cook went ashore. Then before the ship's broker, Arturo Beachie, the cook signed away any share of the money he would have received. The cook also paid his own air fare back to San Diego, California. The captain told us the cook was just happy to get off the boat alive. That evening, the engineer had a big party for the ship's crew ashore at the Union Bar.

The captain then hired a Costa Rican cook who was very good, so we were finally eating well. During the next week we were up in the Gulf of Nicoya catching live bait. Then with a full load of live bait, we were off to Cocos Island and on to the Galapagos Islands.

We would fish all day at Redondo Rock, then head back to Cape Berkely and anchor for the night. After dinner we would sit out on deck, with a glass of cool red wine, and talk about Cookie and how he liked the life of fishing.

Oh yes, the engineer; he smiled and laughed all day, undoubtedly the happiest man I have ever known.

Henry and the "Old Broadbill"

The problem was that the yellowfin tunas just weren't taking the bait. We had plenty of live bait, since the M. V. "Chicken of the Sea" carried 12,000 scoops. We had fished all morning at Redondo Rock in the Galapagos Islands, and had received nothing for our troubles. We sat in the galley, drank coffee and talked to Harold Morgan, the captain.

Since the fishing was no good, we decided to have a day of fun. We headed to Elizabeth Bay, running south and crossing the equator at Cape Berkeley and finally entered Bolivar Channel. We skimmed over the 8 miles between Fernandina and Isabela Islands, then broke out into Elizabeth Bay, which is about 20 miles long and 12 miles wide. The bay is closed in on three sides and is only open to the seas on the west end and through Bolivar Channel. In this beautiful bay, you may find live bait, giant manta rays, sharks, seals and some big broadbill swordfish. Some of the "broadbill" will top 1,000 pounds and stretch more than fifteen feet long. They are good eating, although a little dry.

Our method of catching a broadbill was to use a harpoon. First you found a broadbill; next you got in the work boat, and then came the fun. There are two basic systems used to harpoon a broadbill. One, you circled around him in ever-decreasing circles. Two, you got back a ways and made a high speed run at him, throwing the harpoon as you went by.

On the "Chicken of the Sea," we had some men of Japanese descent, born and raised in the U.S., and one of these was Henry. He was considered by all of us to be one of the nicest men a person could meet. Although he was born and raised in America, his family spoke almost exclusively Japanese, which provided Henry with an accent when he spoke English. He referred to drinking coffee from the "coffee urinal," drinking "agony beer" and he said he had learned things from the "old degeneration." Henry had learned to throw a harpoon from the "old degeneration," so he was our harpoon man.

We ran along with all hands on the bridge looking for our victim. Then, off to starboard, we sighted him. We lowered the work boat into the water; Henry, Bud and Jack jumped in and they were off with a roar.

All of us were on the bridge watching with our binoculars as the work boat started to circle the swordfish. They circled in ever-decreasing circles, until at last, Henry threw the harpoon. But Henry missed the fish. We put the work boat aboard, and we all had a choice word or two about Henry's capability with a harpoon. We were now under way again, looking for another broadbill.

At last we saw one. This broadbill was an old-timer here. He was huge. There were long, gray scars on his side from fighting with sharks. His dorsal fin was broken off, and he just looked mean, ready to fight. Once again the work boat went into the water and our free-spirited fishermen departed.

The crew was on the bridge watching, all eyes focused on Henry. This time, the work boat was away from the fish. It paused a moment, then ran full speed toward the big old-timer. Henry was back from the bow, holding the harpoon like a pool cue. The work boat, making 30 knots, thundered straight for the broadbill. As the work boat passed the giant swordfish, Henry dove over the side, becoming a flying human harpoon. Henry landed on top of the broadbill, but missed with the harpoon. The battle-scarred old-timer didn't want to fight and swam languidly away. Laughing, Captain Morgan slowly lowered his binoculars and turned to us and said, "Now I know why you call him `Kamikaze.'"

Late in the afternoon we pulled into Tagus cove and dropped anchor for the night. After dinner we sat out on deck with a glass of red wine, looking at the names of the old ships that were carved high up on the side of the cliffs. We reminisced about the events of the day, and all agreed that today "Kamikaze" Henry was spectacular.

Dick Latimer Jumps Overboard

Most all of the tuna boats were anchored at Puntarenas, Costa Rica. We were about ten miles southwest of Cape Blanco, which put us about four hours run from the anchorage. The wind was blowing hard, and the seas were running high, the tops of the waves swelling over and making little breaking whitecaps as far as the eye could see. This is why all the other tuna boats were in snug harbor.

We were on board the American Beauty, one of the old bait boats that used live bait. In this type of fishing we would stand in steel racks hooked over the side of the boat, and using a cane pole, catch each fish one at a time. We would fish in the racks, and as the boat rolled we would go down in the water. When the boat rolled hard enough, we would roll under water. We would grab the pipe rack at our knee and hold our breath until the boat rolled the other way. The yellowfin tuna and the sharks, which were attracted by the blood in the water, would swim by in front of us. You could open your eyes under water and look them eye to eye. There have been cases when a shark would grab a fisherman and pull him out of the racks.

We were fishing spinner porpoises, and there was a lot of tuna in the schools. At that time we made, after ship expenses, $11.00 a ton per share. This was big money, and we all wanted to work. Vern, the Captain, called us to the bridge and asked if we wanted to anchor or catch more fish.

We all agreed we wanted to work, so this was the plan. The ship would quarter out of the swell, giving us a slow roll. Next we put the little skiff overboard and towed it with a long line. If, and when, we were washed overboard we could catch the skiff as it went by, if a shark didn't catch us first. We placed a bottle of whiskey and a coffee can with candy and cigarettes in the little skiff and pushed it overboard. The little skiff merrily tracked along behind, and we started into the school of yellowfin.

As we went into the school of tuna, live bait was thrown out, luring the tuna up for the bait. The tuna started taking our hooks, and we were furiously throwing the fish aboard. The ship would roll and we would go under water, holding our breath, then the ship would roll to starboard and we were up for air. When the ship rolled to starboard the ocean water would filter down through the tuna and the bloody sea water would flow out the scuppers. This bloody water, and the fast-moving tuna, excited the sharks. There was plenty of action, and we were making money.

Dick Latimer fished in the corner rack, that is, the first rack. There were two men in each six-foot rack. I was with Dick in the first, and two men were in each rack up the side of the ship. The wind blew, the ship rolled, the tuna came aboard, we were wet and cold but we were making money. We rolled up out of the water and Dick yelled at me, "How'd you like a shot of booze?"

We came up out of the water and I yelled back, "How?"

Dick said, "I'll show ya." With that, he threw his cane pole back inside the ship's railing and jumped overboard. Dick came up astern of us and grabbed the line to the little skiff. As the line ran through his hands, the little skiff came along and Dick pulled himself aboard. I looked back the next time I came up, and there was Dick, taking a long drink out of the whiskey bottle. As I went under on the next roll, I thought about Dick and the booze. We rolled to starboard, and as I came up out of the water, I tossed my pole inboard and jumped overboard.

The tow line slid through my hands, I grabbed the little skiff, and Dick grabbed me. Dick handed me the bottle, and as I took a long drink, I looked at the whitecaps, the rolling ship, and the men in the racks plunging down into the water and coming up again with the next roll. This was living!

About the time of our second pull at the bottle, here came a head alongside. We pulled him in, and as he had a drink, here came another man alongside. We now had four men in the little skiff and the crew on the ship were all throwing their poles inboard and jumping overboard. As Captain Vern signaled "racks up," we pulled in three more men, and then pulled ourselves up to the ship.

We dropped anchor off Puntarenas, Costa Rica, and all hands went ashore. Most of us went into Machalla's restaurant for a steak dinner. The story was told over and over again, about how Dick jumped overboard for a drink of booze.

Harold Hits the Giant Manta

On the old tuna boats, before the net boats, live bait was used to lure the tuna around the boat, that is, wherever we could find yellowfin tuna — in the open ocean, around islands, or off of reefs. Most of the time the bait boats would go to Costa Rica or Panama to look for bait. There were other places to find live bait, also, such as the Gulf of Fonseca and the Galapagos Islands.

The tuna boats would load up with live bait on the coast and take the live bait 600 miles out to Galapagos. On the Chicken of the Sea we carried 12,000 scoops of live bait. On this trip we loaded 12,000 scoops of bait in Panama, appropriated some fresh pineapples, bananas, papaya and coconuts before the irate plantation owner could get to us with his machete, and we were off for Galapagos Islands.

In 1946, Galapagos was virgin country for vast schools of yellowfin tuna, and it was like an old home week at Redondo Rock. Then we made an hour run to Albemarle Reef, on the north end of Isabela Island, and were catching tons of tuna. There were huge sharks here, also. We would shoot the sharks, and sometimes a wounded shark would attack the boat. Some would bite the steel racks, and we would pump more lead into it.

At this reef we would throw out live bait and maybe 50 tons of tuna would come to the boat. We would drift in the three-knot current for several miles, and then the tuna would rush back to the reef. We would throw out a thirty-pound tuna, and a shark would eat it in one gulp.

There were more sharks at Albermarle Reef than in other areas. Albermarle had bluenose and white-tip sharks. Now and then a great white would attack the boat, and this was a sight to behold. When we shot one of these monsters, the other sharks would come in for the kill. We would watch six or eight massive sharks fighting and killing each other.

At the end of a month or so, depending on the amount of tuna, we would be getting low on bait, so we'd have to look for more live bait somewhere in the islands. There was live bait to be found in Elizabeth Bay, Rabida Island, and Sullivan Bay. In this latter bay, behind Bartholome Island, we found thousands of little two-foot sharks on one trip.

On this day we took the Chicken of the Sea down into Elizabeth Bay. There were reports of large schools of Salima, a type of live bait, along the shoreline of Isabela Island. We pulled into 20 fathoms under the keel, and put the rig in the water. The rig consisted of the work boat pulling the big skiff, with the net in it, and the big skiff pulling the little skiff. Daylight broke, and we were off to find Salima.

We found the live bait in about three or four fathoms, circled them and let go the net. When we wrapped the bait, we sometimes also caught predators, like sharks. We wrapped the school, but our net fished seven fathoms deep, and the lead line sometimes tangled in the rocks and lava heads. When that happened, two divers had to put on hard-hat helmets and, as the air was pumped to them by a double-action hand pump, they descended to the bottom. On this trip, I was one of those cold, miserable divers.

I went down with George, my Japanese diving partner, and we slowly closed the lead line. The man in the skiff would pump the air down, and we peered out of a little faceplate. Now and then a big shark would swim by, feeding on the dead bait gilled in the net; he'd eat the net and all.

We just worked along and didn't see the moray eels around us. After about 45 minutes the net was closed, and we climbed into the big skiff, had a shot of booze and lay on the net.

Since we were in shallow water, we couldn't bring the Chicken of the Sea in, so we had to take the live bait out. On bait boats there is an item called a "receiver," which is nothing more than a large box with a bow. The receiver is towed into the net, the live bait is dumped from the net into the receiver, then the work boat slowly tows the receiver back to the tuna boat, and the live bait is transferred onboard.

On this beautiful, clear morning, when the water was like

glass and not a breath of moving air, Harold "Full Throttle" Morgan and Jerry Franks took the work boat back to the Chicken. Harold was driving and he was full ahead. We watched the work boat, making 30 knots, skimming across the deep, blue water with both men standing up. Then came the spectacle.

The work boat stopped dead in the water, two bodies levitated into the air, and we watched these human cannonballs glide like goony birds. These aerial acrobats landed about 40 feet from the work boat, then they slowly swam back to the work boat.

The work boat slowly and laboriously made its way back to the Chicken, where it was hoisted aboard. The crew gathered around, poking and looking. In the end, a new propeller and propeller shaft had to be installed. The work boat came back   three hours later. By this time we had dumped the bait and restacked the net. Finding another school of bait, we made another set and picked up about 1,000 scoops of live bait.

The spectacular enactment of an aerial trajectory that morning had been caused by a giant manta ray. This manta had been sleeping peacefully on the surface of the water when it had been hit by the work boat. These mantas can weigh as much as 3,000 pounds and have a wingspan of twenty feet. You may as well hit a rock. As the sun went down, we pulled into Tagus Cove and anchored.

Tagus is a deep cove surrounded by high cliffs, where the crews of old sailing ships have carved their names and dates. As the evening shadows settled in, we sat on deck and read the names of the old voyagers of the past. We took another sip of our after-dinner drinks, and were grateful to Harold and Jerry for the outstanding display of their maritime talents.

Who Decorated the Pelicans?

Leaving San Diego at about sundown, we passed inside the Coronado Islands and set a course south-southeast for Cedros Island. Passing outside of Cedros, we ran on to Magdalene Bay and went in. Entering "Mag" Bay, we turned to the left and went past the old cemetery and anchored off the little village.

In a short time the big skiff came out from shore and the seven men came aboard. The first to board was the "Comandante," wearing a hat just like General Douglas MacArthur's, then came the six men who rowed the boat. This barefoot crew marched in and, smiling from ear to ear, shook hands all around. Then they told us we would have to pay for coming into their port. This entailed a hot beef sandwich with mashed potatoes and coffee. There was also a bottle of whisky and a carton of cigarettes for the "Comandante."

As old friends, we paid the price and asked how the lobster catch was. They said the catch was poor, but they would go ashore and ask if there were any lobsters.

In a short while the skiff came back, but with a new crew. This "Comandante" told us he was the real "Comandante" and we would now have to pay him. So the cook fed them the sandwiches and the Captain gave out another bottle of whiskey. We asked again about the lobster. This time they asked us how many sacks we wanted, saying there was very much. We wanted six sacks of lobster, we told them, and they left for shore.

The big skiff returned, and this time with them, they had six sacks of lobster. One gunny sack of lobster cost one carton of cigarettes, which was $0.55. With another bottle of whiskey, for friendship, we were underway. We ran past the entrance to "Mag" Bay and into Almejas Bay, also known as Clam Bay for its abundance of very large clams. We went ashore and dug up three gunny sacks of large clams, and as the sun went down we cleared "Mag" Bay and headed southeasterly.

We crossed the Gulf of Lower California, along the shoreline of Mexico, and started into the Gulf of Tehuantepec. A gale force wind was blowing offshore, carrying a lot of sand. We went into Sacrificios Bay and anchored to wait it out. Several of us took our rifles and went ashore to see if we could find a deer or two. We stopped by the big wooden cross on the beach, took one look at the jungle and decided not to hunt. We returned to the boat and as the sun went down, we ate lobster and played poker.

The next day we ran around the Gulf of Tehuantepec in three fathoms, passed Benito lighthouse and were on our way to the Gulf of Fonseca. The shoreline of three countries — El Salvador, Honduras and Nicaragua — border this gulf. Which territorial waters we were in, God only knew. We rounded Amapala Point and anchored in six fathoms. We were anchored in the northern end of the gulf, so we knew we were close to El Salvador. We were close to La Union.

As it was the dark of the moon, we looked for live bait at night. As the school of bait moved through the water, a yellow-green glow was created by the phosphorus in the water. So we ran around all night looking for a yellow-green glow.

When the moon came out or daylight broke, we would return to the tuna boat. During the warm day we would sleep, make up our fishing gear and skim off the dead bait. Since the dead bait was thrown overboard, there were a lot of "freeloaders" — pelicans. Needless to say, there were pelicans all around us, not just in the water, but also on deck. One old fellow even walked into the galley looking for a handout. After a very brief discussion with the cook, he was unceremoniously thrown out.

As there was not a lot to do during the day, one of the crew started to paint in the engine room. The paint was a beautiful, bright red. He painted the deck plates and the ladder, ending up on the main deck. That same old pelican kept coming back in the galley, and he and the cook were going at it again. After a brief period of hand to hand combat, the cook had the pelican down. The engineer with the paint pot took one look and went back to work.

With smiles of glee we threw the pelican overboard and

watched as it paddled right back and climbed aboard. Well, that did it! The pelican war was on. We caught pelicans all day, painting their feet, bills and circles around their eyes. By sundown they were a sight to behold. There must have been sixty or seventy pelicans flying around with red feet, black circles around their eyes and silver bills. On some of them we had varied the color pattern — some had silver feet, red eyes and a black bill. But whatever the pattern, it was a fantastic sight as they walked up and down the deck.

For two more days we had our colorful feathered friends aboard, then we headed back out to sea to find the elusive yellowfin tuna. We ran south and easterly 300 miles off Costa Rica, and that is where we loaded up. With a full load of yellowfin tuna, which would bring in a good payday, we headed back north for San Diego. In the evening as we played cards on the galley table, we had a good laugh about the fantastic sight of the pelicans, and wondered what sort of history an ornithologist would have surmised, had he only been there.

A Dive at Rabida Island

In years gone by, tuna boats were known as bait boats since these fishing boats used live bait to attract a school of yellowfin tuna to them so the tuna could be caught. On this trip I was on the M.V. Corsair, which carried about 330 tons of tuna. We cleared San Diego, and about nine days later arrived at Puntarenas, Costa Rica. Going up into the Gulf of Nicoya, we loaded up with live bait and headed out.

About 25 miles south of Puntarenas is Ballena Bay. We ran into this bay because there is a large plantation of bananas and coconuts. Putting the work boat into the water, some of us went ashore to make an "appropriation."

Some of us went to the banana trees to cut fruit, while others cut down a coconut palm. As the palm tree fell, we yelled "Timber-r-r-r," and all of us ran to the work boat. As we loaded the last coconut on the work boat, along came the plantation owner. Waving his machete and making derogatory remarks about our ancestors, he followed us into the water. By this time we were clear of the beach. Thanking him for his generosity and assuring him our mothers would not run out from under the porch and bite us, we loaded up and departed for Cocos Island.

Cocos Island, a very small island about 290 miles southwest of Costa Rica, may always be found by the rain cloud it hides under. On the northwest side, in its five-mile length, I have counted more than 100 streams of fresh water cascading into the ocean.

As we circled Cocos looking for tuna, we talked about Morgan the pirate and where he hid his treasure. The going idea is that Captain Morgan hid his treasure in a cave which is now under water. Finding neither the treasure nor yellowfin tuna — only a few lonely sharks basking in the sunlight — we set a course for the Galapagos Islands.

We arrived at Culpepper Island and fished along the reef with the beautiful arch sticking up out of the water. Expending about 1,000 scoops of live bait for 50 tons of yellowfin tuna, we sailed the twenty miles to Wenman Island. Finding only some big old sharks, a few manta rays and very few tunas, we then ran the seventy miles to Redondo Rock.

For some strange reason there are always tuna at Redondo Rock. When the tuna would stop biting at Redondo Rock, we would go the twenty miles to Albemarle Point and fish that reef. Fishing was very good and we were loading up fast. We had only one problem; we ran out of live bait. No live bait, no tuna. We talked to Harold Morgan, Captain on the Chicken of the Sea, and as they were out of bait, the decision was made to work together.

We knew there was no bait to be found in Elizabeth Bay, so with a hot tip from Capt. John T. on the White Star, we were off to Rabida Island. The Chicken carried an airplane, which Jerry Franks flew to spot fish for us. Both ships arrived at Rabida by daylight, and Jerry took to the air, looking for live bait. When Jerry would spot fish, he would dive on them and throw out a bolt with a long streamer attached.

Rabida Island is only the cone of an old volcano, less than a mile in diameter, 1,200 feet high, and covered with a weed or two. On the northeast side of this hunk of lava the water is thirty-five fathoms. On the southwest side the strikingly blue depths go down to 300 fathoms. This island was a bad place to find live bait. Jerry flew the airplane around the island looking for bait, while we cruised along slowly, doing the same. At last the airplane went into a dive and as Jerry pulled up, he let a red streamer go.

Finding a school of live bait, we set the net. Henry and I went over the side, put on the diving helmets and started down to close the net. The Galapagos net is built like a huge set of drapes, like the ones you have in your living room. The net fishes about seven fathoms deep. After we circled the bait, two divers have to go down to the lead line at the bottom, and close the net.

The diving helmet weighs 75 pounds, and the air is pumped down to you with a manually operated, double-action hand pump. If the man on the hand pump stops for a cigarette, you just hold your breath until more air comes down. The current of the water drapes the net over you, so you are wrapped in the net, too. If you lose the helmet, you drown!

Henry and I went down, the cold, greenish water changing to a beautiful light blue. There was no such thing as a wetsuit in those days, so we were wet, cold, and gasping for air. There was one little eight-inch glass window to look out of, and you could not bend over without water covering your face.

My teeth chattered from the cold. I peered out of the little glass window and all I saw was light blue water. I was down about seven fathoms, and there wasn't a fish in sight. The bait had sounded and gone under the net to freedom. Henry motioned to surface, so up we went.

Jerry called us on the radio and said he saw them go out under the net. Everyone had an idea and we all talked at once. The decision was made to take the nets of the two ships and sew them together, making one net fourteen fathoms deep, which is about 80 feet.

In about an hour's time we rebuilt the two nets into one deep net. Placing this monster in the big skiff, we were off again. Jerry was up in the airplane spotting bait, while we patrolled below. At last the airplane went into a dive, pulled up and the red streamer sailed down. Circling the live bait, we let go the net and it was closed.

Jerry was landing the airplane when Henry and I went over the side into the cold water. With the 75-pound helmet on, and the air hose under my left arm, I started down into the depths. I looked out the little faceplate and saw Henry going down with me. Once again we were in the wet, cold silence with only the shooo, shooo of the air coming down into the copper helmet. As we passed the seven-fathom mark, the water began to get darker, changing into a deep blue. The water was very clear and extremely cold. I lost sight of Henry, but continued down.

I descended to the bottom of the net, 80 feet down, and hung on the lead line. There was not a fish in sight, not even a shark. The sight was a vast expanse of nothing. Then I felt the net wiggle. I looked off into wet space, and along came another diver.

I watched the other diver work his way along the lead line, then went over to meet him. If you hold these copper helmets together tight, and yell loud enough, we could communicate. We met and I grabbed his helmet and banged mine against his. I peered into his faceplate and saw it was Jerry, the airplane pilot. I yelled as loud as I could, telling him there was nothing here and to surface.

Jerry and I very slowly rose to the surface, the helmets were off, and we were in the big skiff. Our teeth chattered and we shook from the cold, but not enough to stop us from having a good drink of whiskey. Henry had a nosebleed, and that is why he surfaced. Jerry had landed the airplane, and had swum over to the big skiff just as Henry came out of the water. This was the first dive Jerry had made under these conditions.

We loaded the work boat and the big and little skiffs on the Corsair while the crew of the Chicken loaded the airplane. Both ships ran into shallow water by San Salvador Island and anchored for the night. After a dinner of Cabria, lobster tail and white wine, we put the skiff in the water and rowed over to the Chicken. With dry clothes on and a bottle of good booze, I shook hands with the man I had met in fourteen fathoms, in a dive at Rabida Island.

Shootout at Tiger Island

The year was 1946, the big war was over and I was out of the Navy, so now I stood at the end of Tuna Street on Terminal Island, California. Terminal Island is in San Pedro harbor and is home to a lot of tuna boats. I noticed that Mio's Cafe was gone, then across the street I saw the sign Fleet Office, Van Camp Sea Food Co.

I entered the office where the sign said Fleet Manager, and a large man behind a big desk asked, "Well, what do you want, kid?"

I told him I wanted to go fishing, and he laughed. I looked at him and he laughed at me. "Did you ever fish before?" I answered in the positive and he stopped laughing. "What boat?"

"The Sea Boy," I answered with a smile. Tex Ellington, for that was his name, then asked me who was the skipper. I told him Vern Bowman and Walter Morgan ran the boat. Mr. Ellington then informed me they had a new boat at Crag Shipyard, and were looking for a crew.

I drove over to Crag Shipyard, climbed up the ladder and stood on the deck of the M.V. American Beauty. The Beauty was a two-masted brine boat built by George and Dave Campbell in San Diego. The old Sea Boy was an ice boat; that is, you packed each fish by hand in ice. The Beauty used a new system; you put the fish in a tank of water, added rock salt and froze the tuna with a liquid brine. Modern technology!

As I stood on deck, Walter Morgan came out of the engine room. He rounded the corner, saw me and yelled, "Well, S— B——, if it isn't the kid! Are you looking for a job? You're hired." We sat down to the galley table with a cup of black coffee, and I told him what I had been doing for the last four years. Walt told me that he and Vern often wondered what happened to me and agreed if I ever came back I had a job. I signed on the American Beauty, and a month later we headed south.

We picked up some live bait at Cedros Island and went up into the Gulf of Lower California. Finding no yellowfin tuna there, we headed on down the coast of Mexico. We skirted the Gulf of Tehuantepec in three fathoms, just outside the breaker line, and sailed past Guatemala. Arriving at the Gulf of Fonseca we rounded Amapala Point and were now in the Gulf.

The Gulf of Fonseca is bounded by three countries — El Salvador, Honduras and Nicaragua — with no boundary markers in the water, so God only knew what country you were in. We were just off El Salvador, by Tiger Island.

We did not have a full load of live bait and our main purpose here was to catch some. It was the dark of the moon, so we caught the bait at night. We would put the work boat in the water and drag the big and little skiff behind, looking for a school of live bait.

On a dark night, when there is plenty of phosphorus in the water, any movement of water makes a yellow-greenish glow. When the bait moved, the glow gave it away, and we set the net on this.

All night long we would run around the Gulf and set the net on a yellow-green glow. We would pull the net in by hand, bail the catch into the wells on the Beauty, then do it again. When the moon came out or daylight broke, we tied the rig behind the Beauty and anchored.

During the warm day we would sleep, make up our fishing gear, and take care of the live bait. Some of the bait would die, so we would skim it off and throw it to the pelicans and shark. We were even known to heat potatoes in the oven, and feed them to the sharks.

We had about four days of this fun and frolic, then on the afternoon of the fifth day we watched a small sail boat approach. The deck watch called the Captain, and one by one we picked up our binoculars and watched. I counted eleven men in the boat. Then I saw they had rifles. The Captain gave the order to pull the anchor, start the main engine and stand by to maneuver.

The small boat blocked our way to the open ocean, so we slowly circled Tiger Island and came out the south end. As the small boat drew closer, we went full ahead and pulled away. They were about 200 yards off, when they fired the first shot. We had the ship's flags flying, so there was no mistake who we were. They had no flag up and they had opened fire on us.

Their fire was continuous and we hid behind the bait tank. The Captain gave the order to return their fire. As most of us were veterans of the late war, we were well armed. We now returned their fire, and the war was on.

Clearing the reef just south of Tiger Island, we headed for the open ocean. With a few parting shots, we were once again on the high seas and bound for Costa Rica.

We fished our way down the coast and went into Puntarenas, Costa Rica for a fishing permit. With a full load of live bait, we ran on down the coast, finishing off our load by the islands of Jicarita, Jicaron and Coiba.

With a full load of yellowfin tuna, we set a course northwesterly up the coast, and headed home. When there was nothing else to do, we would sit at the galley table and play poker. We found several bullet holes in the Beauty on the starboard side. Could they have been Government men? Why didn't they have a flag up? Why did they shoot at us? Maybe they were pirates looking for an American tuna boat. Plunging into the swells, homeward bound, we sat around the galley table and often talked of the shootout at Tiger Island.

Stay Inside or Get Shot

It was a warm, pleasant evening, with a tropical rain shower now and then. I was sitting with a friend of mine in the Union Bar in Puntarenas, Costa Rica having dinner with two of the young ladies who inhabited this den of iniquity. There were perhaps twenty-five or thirty other patrons of the establishment indulging in their various pastimes when, with a great deal of noise and rattling of sabers, in marched the army.

What took place next was fast and furious. Some of the men were knocked down by the army, while the girls went screaming into the shadows of the night. Then standing beside me, with a drawn saber, was an army officer. He had the typical military scrambled eggs on his hat and, remembering that silence is golden, I sat there as if mummified. He looked at me and I looked at him. Obviously, we were two Americans having dinner.

"Usted parte de la revolucion?" he asked me in Spanish. We were not part of the revolution. We were here as part of the crew on the tuna boat American Beauty. The "General" told us to stay inside because it would be a bad night to be out. We could hear a few shots now and then, sporadically, and then silence.

My shipmate and I stayed in the Union Bar listening to the rain on the tin roof, and the intermittent shooting. By 1:00 A.M. there was silence about the town, broken only by the sound of the army patrol marching up and down the streets.

There had not been a shot fired for about two hours. I would look outside every half-hour, peering up and down the street, and saw only the six-man army patrol outside. The patrol marched by about every half-hour, and that helped us form our plan. The next time a patrol came by, we would march off with them.

We stood in the doorway and watched; here they came. The patrol passed by with only a glance at us, and we fell in step behind them. The last two men looked at us, but said nothing. We all marched down the block in the light rain. After marching about ten blocks, we turned toward the ocean, the side where the pier is located. Stepping right along, we arrived on the waterfront and turned toward the pier. Lady Luck was still with us.

In the wee hours of the morning and in a drizzling rain, we marched past the pier head. As we marched by, Dick and I made a right turn onto the pier and hotfooted it to the end. This pier is "L"-shaped, and there was a lot of cargo waiting to be loaded. Dick and I hunkered down behind some large cases and waited.

About every half-hour a work boat from one of the tuna boats came by to pick up late crew members. Our luck was still holding, for here came a boat. We yelled, stood up in the dim light on the end of the pier, and the boat came in. I yelled to the boat that we would jump in the water and to pick us up. He waved and we jumped.

The work boat picked us up and took us to the American Beauty. And so ended another quiet night ashore in Costa Rica.

Collision at Sea

With my hands in my pockets, I walked down the embarcadero in San Diego. I was looking for a job as navigator on a tuna boat, and someone told me that George Soares was looking for one. Captain Soares owned the Judy S, which I thought must be named after his wife or daughter. I pulled up short beside the Judy S. and looked her over. She was an old bait boat. I had sailed on better, but I thought - why not?

I scrambled down to the main deck, where the galley was, and went in. There was a raunchy cook peeling potatoes. Why I didn't know. Everyone usually ate ashore. In broken English, he offered me a cup of coffee, I thanked him and asked for the captain. He told me the captain was in the engine room, so that's where I headed.

I found Captain Soares, and we went back into the galley for a cup of bad coffee. George Soares spoke excellent English, and in a very few minutes I liked him. Evidently, the feeling was mutual, so I signed on for the trip. I took a turn around and looked the boat over. She was an older bait boat, but looked solid to me. The next day I put my gear on board.

We took about three days to outfit the Judy S., and as the sun went down we cleared San Diego Bay, around the last of August of 1950. Henry was the chief engineer, and he never backed off from a drink in his life. We cleared the Coronado Islands and I set a course for outside Cedros Island.

George told me to head for the Galapagos Islands directly, outside of the Gulf of Tehuantepec. From outside Cedros Island to Culpepper Island, Galapagos, is a direct line. I set the course and let the automatic pilot do the rest. Due to ocean currents, a ship will set out westerly for a few days. Then the current will set you back easterly about the same amount. I would take the star sights in the morning and evening for a fix, and would not change course. On the day of arrival I scanned the horizon for a cloud near the bow. When I saw the cloud, I surreptitiously changed the auto-pilot, so we're heading for the cloud. When an island appeared on the horizon, the crew thought I was a great navigator.

Culpepper Island is a rock that sticks up out of the ocean, but there is a beautiful arch that seemed to always have yellowfin tuna near it. As yet we didn't have any live bait, so we ran on past Wenman Island down to Isabela Island. Taking Bolivar Channel, between Isabela and Fernandina Islands, we arrived in Elizabeth Bay.

This bay is about fifteen by twenty-five miles square, with a deep cove at the southeast corner. In this cove, which is Perry's Isthmus, there are very shallow soundings, submerged rocks and reefs. There are also schools of salima, which the fisherman catch to use as live bait. This live bait, in turn, is put in bait tanks on the tuna boat and is then used to lure the yellowfin tuna to the boat. This is the system used to catch yellowfin tuna. Bluefin are not caught in quantity with this system.

We pulled into Perry's Isthmus and put the work boat, net boat and the small skiff in the water. Going into three fathoms of water, we searched the shallow soundings for the elusive salima. In short order we found a school of live bait and, setting the net, we apprehended them immediately. In two days we loaded up with enough live bait to start after the yellowfin tuna. We ran north, between Fernandina and Isabella Islands, around Cape Berkeley and then the seventeen miles to Redondo Rock.

Redondo Rock jets up from about seventeen hundred fathoms, or 10,200 feet, in just a radius of about four miles. There is a one to two-knot current of cooler water passing by it all of the time, which seems to attract the tuna. Tuna can be either one-pole, two-pole or three-pole. The largest tuna I ever landed from the "Rock" was 360 pounds. We were three-poling when this monster took the hook. Six of us rolled him into the rack. He stuck out a foot or two on each end. The standard rack is six feet long.

We worked along for several weeks, going in to anchor at night behind Cape Berkeley. About this time George's brother, Joe Soares, came in and anchored. George and I went over and talked with him all evening about the fishing conditions and where to find live bait. This was Joe's first trip to Galapagos.

Daylight broke clear, the air was fresh, just a beautiful day when we rounded Cape Berkeley, northbound. Someone looked back off the port stern, and there was a breezing school of tuna. A breezing school might be a hundred tons of tuna that surface for a few minutes, and then all of a sudden sound.

We turned to a southerly course and slowed down. The breezing school was boiling with big tuna — three-pole! We lowered the racks, got our three-pole rigs and waited for George to bring us into the school. The engine stopped, and so did the vibration. The chummer on the bait tank started throwing out the live bait. With the tuna boiling alongside, we were in the racks. All of us hooked up at the same time. The tunas were in a frenzy, biting at anything in the water. I was lead man in our three-man team, and when we hooked up I pulled back. So did the other two men, and we tore the hook out of the fish's mouth.

Someone was yelling, "Don't pull so hard. Their mouths are soft. Easy, easy." When our lure hit the water, a big tuna grabbed it immediately. We pulled the monster aboard, and then I had a good look at him. This tuna was a different type of fish than I had ever seen.

The first thing I noticed was the eye. It was huge, almost twice the size of a normal yellowfin. This tuna looked like a gigantic albacore squeezed into a shorter model. The pectoral fin was extremely long and folded into a groove like an albacore. The fish had a very soft mouth. It wasn't built like a yellowfin or a bluefin tuna. These fish would run about one hundred and fifty pounds; it was hard to get them aboard using a three-pole rig.

We loaded up the deck, which would be about fifteen tons, and by this time the school sounded. Captain Soares put the ship slow ahead, and we took a good look at our catch. This tuna was a different type of tuna, not yellowfin or bluefin.

We all ran up to the bridge to look for another breezing school. Several of the older fisherman had seen this type of tuna before.

They explained that the Japanese call them "Big Eye," while the Portuguese called them "Patuki." Whatever it was, it was a different type of tuna.

We were running dead slow, about five miles southwest of Cape Berkeley, looking for another breezing school. The tuna boat Sun King was in the area, looking for tuna, also. We spotted a breezing school and turned toward it. About the same time, the Sun King turned toward the school. They headed in from our port side, which gave us the right-of-way.

I was down in the galley talking with the cook when I felt our engine stop and then go astern. I looked out the port side, and here came the Sun King. Thinking this was really going to be close, I ran up to the bridge. George was blowing the danger signal on the ship's air horn, the engine was going astern, and the crews of both ships were straggling out onto the forward deck to see the fun.

George told me to start writing in the ship's log, and be sure to mark the time every five minutes. I was writing in the ship's log, entering the time and watching us come closer together. In a few minutes George yelled at me, "Watch this!"

When the men in the crew saw we were really going to hit, they backed away from the bow. Very slowly, almost like a dream, we hit the Sun King. The Judy S. rammed into the Sun King about twenty feet aft of the starboard bow.

In slow motion, the Sun King, which was a steel boat, rolled to her port side. The Judy S., which was a wooden ship, lifted up slightly. As the deck plates of the Sun King slowly buckled and the steel crumpled in, the Judy S. came to a dead stop.

Very slowly we backed away from the Sun King, and George stopped the engine. George asked Henry, our engineer, to look below for damage. We lay to while the men on the Sun King looked for damage, and our crew did, also. Apparently there was no damage below the water line on either ship, so with a lot of yelling in Portuguese, we got under way.

The accident was September 20, 1950 at Galapagos Islands. On March 8, 1951, I was called by the insurance company to fill out a report of an accident. Both captains were licensed, but I held the only other deck officer's license. You might say that I had the "swing vote."

We were under way, and looking for a breezing school. In a few minutes one surfaced, and we were back in the racks pulling big fish again. The tunas were of the same type, albacore squeezed down with huge eyes. During this day there were various schools of these strange tunas that surfaced and we took out tonnage. These tunas were in breezing schools, and just north of Fernandina Island, Galapagos.

We saw these tunas on this one day, and never again. We took about sixty tons of these fish aboard, and then finished the load at Redondo Rock. Nothing was ever said about these odd fish. No one called Scripps School of Oceanography. I looked in the National Geographic Book, Wondrous World of Fishes — nothing.

I don't remember how many tons of fish the Judy S. carried, but we had a full load when we left Galapagos. I think we refueled in Costa Rica, then headed up the coast to San Diego, California. I was on the scales at the cannery, representing the fisherman, so I know these strange tunas averaged out well more than one hundred pounds each.

We cleaned up the Judy S. so she was as we had found her. I packed my sea bag and, along with my old guitar, walked up the pier. George Soares was at the pier head with our paychecks. A full share was eleven dollars a ton, after subtracting the expenses of the trip. We had three hundred tons, after expenses, and with a big smile George handed me a check for three thousand and three hundred dollars. Not bad, for a little less than three months work.

With my check in my pocket, I bid farewell to George Soares and another trip to the Galapagos Islands. This trip had been a little different. There were those big, three-pole, funny-looking tuna, the "Big Eye" or "Patuki." Or, could they have been the fish called "Allison's Tuna?" Then there was another `first' — a collision at sea.

False Teeth in the Pie

After WWII — the Big One, that is — I obtained a job on the M. V. American Beauty, one of the new brine boats built by George and Dave Campbell, of the Campbell Shipyard. In this year of 1946, the American Beauty was one of the better tuna boats. She carried 330 tons, 15 men in the crew including a great cook. These tuna boats, or bait boats as they were called, fished for yellowfin tuna and used live bait to lure in the tuna.

First we had to find the live bait, and next we had to apprehend these crafty little critters. We traveled along 2,000 miles of coastline, from San Diego, California to the Gulf of Panama. After catching the live bait, we placed them in bait wells on the tuna boat and then wandered more than a thousand miles of open ocean, including islands, reefs and sea mounts, looking for yellowfin tuna.

On these trips we were at sea about three months, so we had to have personalities that would work in close quarters for a long period of time. We were now out about six weeks and, having loaded up with live bait in Costa Rica, were now fishing the Galapagos Islands. We would fish Redondo Rock all day, then run twenty miles to Cape Berkeley and anchor for the night, returning next morning back to the Rock. My watch partner and I had the three-to-six watch, so we took care of the navigation. We navigated with a sextant and utilized 250 stars, plus the sun, moon and planets

After we were anchored, we still had the three-to-six watch. We would watch the bait, the swing of the ship and with a cup of coffee in hand, lean on the ship's rail and watch the stars. To go along with the coffee, there was always cake, pie or some other pastry. Our ship's cook was a retired navy baker and he turned out the pastry in real production.

Now one of the owners of the Beauty was Walter Morgan. Walt was a huge man with a heart of gold, a ready grin, and false teeth. When we had the evening meal, Walt would never eat his dessert. He would put this pastry in the refrigerator to eat with his morning coffee. The only trouble was, he didn't get up till daylight, and by then Jack and I had already eaten his pastry.

The entire crew would be standing around drinking coffee when Walt entered the galley. Walt would draw a cup of coffee, set it on the table, and go to the refrigerator. He would open the door, look in and find his pastry gone. He would then go into a tirade about anyone who would eat his pastry. You might say that Walt had a meticulously articulate vocabulary of four-letter descriptive adjectives. This morning's drama had gone on for several weeks, always the same. Jack and I ate his pastry!

We fished all day at Redondo Rock then crossed the equator at Cape Berkeley, traveled a few more miles and anchored in a beautiful, sheltered bay. We had a gourmet dinner of lobster tail, sea bass with red and white wine. Then, to our delight, the cook brought out some lemon meringue pies. Cutting the pies into very large pieces, this masterpiece was placed before us.

A gigantic piece of lemon meringue pie was placed before Walt. The meringue had to be two inches deep and all eyes were watching. Walt slowly stood up, looked up and down the galley table, then glowering at all of us, he snarled, "Anybody touch this pie, I'll kill 'em."

There was silence about the deck. No one moved. You could hear the lapping of the water on the side of the ship. Walt looked up and down the table again and, as an afterthought, took out his upper false teeth and mashed them into the meringue, embedding them securely. Walt then flounced over to the refrigerator and placed his pie inside.

I looked at Jack, and our minds locked on only one thought. In the wee hours of the morning, that piece of pie would vanish from the face of the earth. As the cards were dealt for the evening's poker game, Jack and I smiled with glee.

We relieved the watch at 0300, took a look around and headed for the galley. The engineer was below and Jack and I were the only ones on deck. Walt was sound asleep in his room. I opened the refrigerator door and surreptitiously withdrew Walt's piece of pie. I set this creation, with the false teeth mashed in, on the galley table. Jack brought a knife, fork and spoon as I set coffee cups on the table. With a sip of coffee, Jack and I scrutinized this masterpiece of culinary art.

Structurally, the bending of the false teeth would stabilize the pie from falling over. The lemon was solid and the meringue was hard. Like two brain surgeons performing a delicate operation, Jack and I dissected the lemon meringue pie.

As Jack and I sipped on our coffee, with great care we carved away first the meringue, then the lemon pie. Spoonful by spoonful we removed all of the material from around the teeth. In the end we had the false teeth embedded in the meringue on top of a cliff of yellow lemon pie. Bubbling over with joy, we put the dish with its sparse contents back in the refrigerator and went out on deck to watch the daylight break and call the crew.

Once again we were under way to Redondo Rock. The crew was up and filing into the galley for breakfast when Walt walked in. He drew a cup of coffee, then walked to the refrigerator. Jack and I sat by the galley door so we could vacate the area in case of a disaster.

Walt opened the door, looked inside at his teeth and once again there was silence about the decks. We were once again amazed and entranced by Walter's command of the short-lettered words in the English language. I inferred that all of our forefathers had been bachelors, and if and when we ever got home, our mothers would run out from under the porch and bite us in the leg. As the air turned blue and the four-letter words flowed out of Walt's mouth, Jack and I hastily vacated the galley and went up on the bridge.

Two-pole tunas were breaking around the boat, and we were down in the racks pulling them aboard. Walt was up on the bait tank, throwing out live bait, and Jack and I could still hear him expounding about someone that would eat all of his pie, and leave only his false teeth.

Adrift at Sea

This is the tale that was told to me by the man with the crystal eye. Although I never sailed on this tuna boat, I did know all of the people involved. This event took place before World War II, on the "Old" Chicken of The Sea, and in later years was told around the fishing docks.

In the early years of tuna fishing, when the boats only fished off the coast of Mexico, the Morgan family — Pop, Walter and Donald Morgan — went into the business with an old boat called the "Morgan," which I think was a converted sub chaser.

In the 1930's, the Morgan family purchased another tuna boat and named it `Chicken of The Sea'. This was the first `Chicken', not to be confused with the Chicken of The Sea built at Birchfield Boiler Works in Washington State. That was built in 1942 and was 502 gross tons. This story is about the old, wooden Chicken of The Sea.

By this time the tuna boats, the ones that used live bait and caught the tuna using poles, were exploring as far south as the Galapagos Islands. The Chicken was a family-operated vessel, run by the six Morgans that I know of — Pop, Walt, Donald and then Pop's three boy's Harold, Bud and Melvin.

The Chicken had picked up a load of live bait in Costa Rica, looked around Cocos Island and then went on to the Galapagos Islands. With Pop as the captain and Tex Ellington as engineer, all the rest fished down in the racks. The work was hard, with long hours in the racks, soaking wet, but at last they finished the load.

With a prolonged blast of the ship's whistle, they headed toward Cocos Island. Bud, Harold and Tex worked in the engine room while Pop, Walt, and Melvin worked the deck watch. There were one or two others working in each capacity, but basically this was the crew. Bud Morgan was a real alcoholic . . . not a drunk, but an alcoholic. He would drink a quart a day and work right along with the others. The rest of the men in the engine room just liked a drink now and then.

Pop Morgan had control of the booze and he stopped the flow. There was to be no drinking on the ship, he declared. This is where the trouble began. By the time the old Chicken was halfway between Cocos and Galapagos Islands the trouble came to a head.

Bud went up to the bridge and asked his dad, Pop, for a bottle of whiskey. Pop turned him down, cold flat. Bud went back down to the engine room and Tex came up to the bridge. Tex had a long talk with Pop, but Pop held firm — no booze. Tex went back to the engine room and the 'black gang' huddled together hatching a plan.

They decided they would all go to the bridge and take a bottle of whiskey. Some went up one side, while others went up the other side of the ship. As Pop's boy, Harold, arrived at the top of the ladder, Uncle Walt hit him in the eye, knocking him back down to the main deck. Harold had a bloody nose, a beautiful black eye and was madder than a wet cat.

A general fight ensued, with a lot of pushing and shoving and a few more black eyes. In the end, Pop still had the booze and the 'black gang' went below to pout.

Surreptitiously, the 'black gang' went up to the galley and took a lot of food down to the lower engine room. They had enough food for a week and, of course, they had a pipe for fresh water. Then they barricaded the doors leading into the engine room. When everything was ready, they stopped the main engine, putting the ship adrift.

Pop and Walt went down to the door leading into the engine room and yelled and hollered at Bud and Tex, but to no avail. Bud yelled back, "No booze, no engine." So there they drifted, halfway between Cocos and Galapagos Islands.

These men were all exceptionally strong-willed. Eventually the Morgan family owned other tuna boats. Tex became Fleet Manager for Van Camp Sea Food while Harold was in charge of the Samoa operation for Van Camp. Donald Morgan had his own ship and lived in Costa Rica. He is the one that cleaned out the sharks, for their livers, in the Gulf of Nicoya, Costa Rica. But for now, these hardheaded men were drifting at sea.

As the story goes, they drifted out there for three days and two nights. At last Pop made a deal with Bud and gave them a case of whiskey. When the `black gang' had the case of whiskey below in the engine room, they started the main engine and the ship got underway. As long as Bud, Tex and Harold had whiskey, the Chicken would not be adrift at sea.

.

Big Fish on the Lawn

The Archipelago De Colon, better known as the Galapagos Islands, lies on the equator, about six hundred miles west of Ecuador. It comprises about sixteen islands, ranging from the large island that is seventy miles long, to various little islands of one mile in length.

After World War II, these islands, which belong to Ecuador, were the fishing grounds for the tuna boats out of San Diego, California. The islands were virgin country for yellowfin tuna that ranged in size from small to huge. This is a story of two of the latter.

In 1947, I was one of the crew of the M. V. American Beauty, a two-masted, 330-ton capacity wooden fishing boat captained by Vernon Bowman. Most all of the sixteen man crew were veterans of World War II, single, and were a rowdy bunch in general. The work was hard and dangerous, but we didn't know any better. By the death benefits we paid to the union, there were about twenty-five deaths a year. The insurance rates were the second highest in the United States, being second only to coal miners.

The American Beauty cleared San Diego, arriving in Puntarenas, Costa Rica nine days later. The port of Puntarenas, situated on a sand spit, is at the mouth of the Gulf of Nicoya. Up in this gulf were immense schools of live bait, which we would spend a week catching, and then we'd haul the live bait to various islands, reefs and sea mounts, including the Galapagos Islands.

Loading up with about eight thousands scoops of live bait, the Beauty cleared Costa Rica and headed for the Galapagos Islands. As Cocos Island was on our course for Galapagos, naturally we took a turn around the island, looking for fish. There were a lot of sharks but no tuna, so we set a course for the Galapagos Islands.

A little less that a day and a half later, we arrived at Culpepper Island, the northernmost island of the group. Throwing live bait out along the reef with the beautiful stone arch, we found nothing, so headed for Wenman Island. With a lack of yellowfin tuna and an abundance of large sharks around Wenman Island, we departed for Redondo Rock, a distance of seventy miles.

Redondo Rock is a big, flat pinnacle of a seven-thousand-foot submerged mountain. This little hundred acres, flat rock sticks out of the water about two hundred and twenty feet, but the surrounding area abounds with all sizes of yellowfin tuna. The big tunas were there today. These tunas were what we called three-pole or four-pole tuna. Three men would bridle the lines of their eleven-foot cane fishing poles together, so there was only one hook in the water. The same with four-pole fishing. The tuna would run about two hundred and fifty pounds. If you were hit by one, you might as well be hit by a Charger linebacker.

On this beautiful, clear day, with mild seas and drenched in sunlight, we were fishing three-pole tuna. Jack Vore, Henry Shamada and I were the team fishing in the stern rack of the Beauty. Vernon Bowman and Walter Morgan were up on the bait tank, throwing out live bait. These massive tunas were pulled aboard.

We would fish for a while, then the ocean current would carry us away from the Rock. Vern would run up to the bridge, start the engine and circle back to the Rock. We, in turn, would move the tuna from the deck and place them into a fish well. The Beauty would slow down, live bait would be thrown out, and once again the large tuna would come up to bite the hooks.

Our three-man team, fishing in a stern rack, was throwing in the tuna with a rhythm. The fish were biting at a regular interval, and we were talking about something unimportant when one took the hook. I pulled back with the other two men, but nothing moved. As I looked down at the fish, my pole broke, but what I saw was astounding.

With the three of us pulling, the only thing protruding out of the water was the nose of the fish. The four-inch eye of the tuna was just even with the water; nothing was moving. As I grabbed the line from my pole, I could hear men yelling, "Help those men! My God, get that fish aboard!"

The three men in the corner rack came in our rack to help. With know-how and hooks we rolled the giant tuna into our six-foot steel rack. This yellowfin tuna protruded about two feet off each end of the rack. It was a real monster! The fish was about nine feet long and the largest I had ever seen on deck.

With a new three-pole rig, we were once again fishing. Within five minutes, a brother of the one we caught bit the hook of the corner rack team. Once again everyone yelled, and we jumped in their rack and helped them pull the giant tuna aboard.

We pulled these two immense tunas forward, by the galley. All of us sat there and admired our huge catch. At the end of about an hour, one fish gave a gigantic flip of its tail, no more.

With a lot of pulling and tugging, laced with foul language, we placed the fish in one of the refrigerated cargo holds to be frozen. In another week we finished our load and, with a prolonged blast on the whistle to say goodbye to the other boats, we headed north. With a stopover in Manzanillo, Mexico, for fuel, we finished the trip in San Diego, California.

Vern brought the American Beauty alongside the dock at the Van Camp Sea Food Cannery at the foot of Crosby street. As it was late in the afternoon, we were told to start unloading at 0600 in the morning. Jack and I had a room at Top's Motel, on Pacific Coast Highway, so we cleaned up and had a night on the town.

The next morning we started unloading. In those days we did our own work; we never hired anyone to replace us for unloading. Jack Vore was watching the weight scales, to keep the cannery honest, and he said the tuna's average weight was two hundred and forty pounds. We were placing three fish to the loading bucket. In the late afternoon, we pulled out our two prize monsters. With great pride we placed a sling around their tails and swung them ashore.

The fish inspector, in his white smock and clipboard under his arm, walked around our enormous tuna, shaking his head. We stood there admiring our catch, expecting praise from the inspector. Instead, he stopped, turned around, and with a sneer on his lips said, "Rejected!"

Rejected! That's almost eight hundred pounds of yellowfin tuna! We finished the day unloading tuna, while our pride and joy lay out in the sun and thawed. The sun went down and we gathered in the galley. There was plenty of booze on the table, and our precious fish were still laying on the dock. We talked about what a rotten deal. The inspector didn't like our beautiful monsters. Then we came up with a great idea.

We would all meet on the dock at midnight. I had dinner on the American Beauty and stretched out in my bunk to rest. When midnight rolled around, we were all on the dock. Several of the members of the crew had pickup trucks, so we loaded the huge tuna into two trucks, one fish in each truck. Their tails stuck out the end. In high spirits we drove to the address of the inspector, in National City. One of the crew had scouted out the house, so we drove right up in front.

We had planned this little party out in detail. Not a sound. Drive up, pull out the fish, place them on the lawn and leave. We did exactly that. We put those massive tunas on the front lawn of the inspector. If he wouldn't buy them, then we would give them to him. We went to our various homes or motels and called it a night.

The next morning we were unloading tuna by 0600, but there was a different inspector. About noon our regular inspector arrived onboard the ship. He had a story to tell, but by now he was laughing.

As we ate our noon meal in the galley, the inspector told us his story. He said that he was up at 0500, was going to have a cup of coffee and come over to the cannery. He had finished his coffee and was on his way out to his car when he saw the cats.

The inspector said there were millions, but when we pinned him down, there were only about twenty. He called some of his neighbors, telling them they could have all of the tuna they wanted. His friends came over and cut away huge chunks of tuna to take home, but only about one hundred pounds was packed out by the neighbors.

Finally, at about nine o'clock he called a butcher. The butcher said he didn't want the fish, because it was uninspected. The price was right, but if the butcher was caught, what kind of fine would be incurred? The inspector told the butcher that he was an inspector and would write a letter concerning the fish. In the end, the inspector had to pay the butcher to cut up the two tunas and take them away.

By the time the inspector finished telling this story we were all howling with glee. Toward the end, even the inspector was laughing. The last thing he said was, "Never in my life have I had a fish put on my lawn, much less monsters like that!"

Pappy and The Deer

As I looked out the window of the boat, the rain beat hard on the glass pane, and the swell seemed to have changed. On an easterly wind, I could smell the jungle, so I turned on the fathometer. We had passed over the hundred-fathom curve, and daylight would break in a little while.

The weather was making up, so we left Guardian Bank, about 110 miles west-southwest of Costa Rica, and were heading into Braxilito Bay. Fishing for the elusive yellowfin tuna on the old bait boats took us from Mexico to Ecuador, and also all of the islands and shallow soundings.

Guardian Bank is a tough place to fish, not only because of its position, but also because of the size of the tuna. We could usually find yellowfin here, but the size would vary. There would be a school of twenty-pound tuna, which requires one pole, or one man to land. Then all of a sudden the school would change to fifty-pound tuna. Now they are two-pole tuna, requiring two men using one hook. Next along could come a school of hundred-pound tuna. Now we'd need three men to one hook, also known as three-poling. By the time we were fishing with four poles and one hook, the fish are running about one hundred and fifty to two hundred pounds. With the size of the fish constantly changing, this area was a bad place to work. A lot of men were hurt here.

If the men are fishing one pole, or twenty-pound tuna, and a hundred-pound tuna came along, a man could be pulled over the side. Because of the sharks, who were excited by the blood in the water, that man could lose his life.

My watch on the boat was 0300 to 0600, because I took care of the navigation. During my watch, I could take star sights in the early morning and early evening. We passed over the fifty-fathom curve, and I changed course more to the north. The smell of the wet, rotting jungle was stronger now. The incessant rain was still coming down as I went below for a hot cup of coffee, and to call the captain. On this trip, Melvin Morgan was the captain, and I was on the M.V. Corsair. The Corsair fished for Van Camp

Seafood, and could carry 330 tons of tuna.

Just after daylight, we dropped anchor in Braxilito Bay, south of Cape Velas, Costa Rica. This bay has jungle along the shoreline, but beautiful sandy beaches. I scrutinized the hills, and there were open clearings with lots of tall grass. A good-sized stream of fresh water flowed into the bay out of a dark canyon. I called "Pappy" Tucker, our Chief Engineer, and together we looked over the hill country. Pappy and I had made many a hunt together, and now we wanted to hunt in Costa Rica.

Making up a little lunch in a knapsack, we took our deer rifles and went ashore in the small skiff. Stepping out on the white, sandy beach fifty yards up from the stream, we pulled the skiff high up in the sand. Then, shouldering our rifles, we started into the jungle.

Pappy took the lead and, watching for snakes, we slowly made our way toward a small hill. We had looked at the country with binoculars from the bridge of the Corsair, so we had a good idea where we were going. Now we wanted to get in the tall grass. With the fresh water near by, there should be deer, also.

From the ship, we had seen a grassy ridge that ran almost down to the bay, and this is where we were headed. After struggling through a hundred yards of jungle we started up the ridge. We broke out of the jungle and very slowly moved up the ridge. One man would move while the other would watch, never both moving at the same time. We worked our way up this ridge for perhaps half a mile, then low and to our right emerged a large, flat meadow. Pappy and I separated, then knelt on one knee in a ready-to-shoot position.

We knelt motionlessly in the knee-high grass, like two stone statues. After maybe fifteen minutes, a small forked horn stood up. We had previously agreed that Pappy would shoot first, then if he missed, I would shoot. Pappy sighted through the buck horn sights, on his old 30-40 Krag, and pulled the trigger. The deer went down as if hit by a building. Pappy threw another shell in the chamber, and we both watched. As the sound echoed across the hills, Pappy said, "Right through the heart. Deader than a mackerel." With that statement, a little forked horn jumped up, and was off on a dead run.

I fired, then Pappy fired, both of us missing. The deer was out of sight in a small canyon running off of the grassy flat.

We moved slowly down to where we had last seen the deer. The grass was knee-high, and they have some bad snakes in this country, so we stepped very slowly. I picked up the tracks of the little buck, and followed for thirty yards. Not a drop of blood. That deer was running in good shape, and had never been hit.

Backtracking up the gully, we came out on the flat once again. We tracked along the flat until we came to the deer's bed, and there lay the little buck. There had been two deer; they must have been brothers. Pappy shot the first, and then the second jumped up. That was the deer that ran down the canyon.

We field dressed the deer and looked around the country. The best way to get out was to go up to the ridge. So, while Pappy carried the rifles and led the way, I packed the deer. I turned up the collar on my shirt, carrying the deer high on my shoulders. We made the ridge and sat down to rest. Looking around, we decided to go down to the freshwater stream and follow it out. I shouldered the deer and we started down to the stream.

After twenty yards of jungle, we came to the stream. The water was only knee-deep, so we walked in and started downriver. By now the bugs and various flying critters were swarming around the dead deer. I didn't mind the critters biting the deer, but they gnawed on me, too. The stream narrowed, and we were well over our knees in water. We broke out onto the sandy beach, and made the short walk to our skiff. We then both jumped in the bay. After washed the flying critters out of our hair and off our clothing, we rowed out to the ship.

With the deer cooling, Pappy and I jumped in a bait tank and cleaned up. I had two wood ticks on my neck, which were gorging themselves with my blood. You cannot pull them out, but a little touch of camphor oil will make them back out to meet their timely death.

That night, the crew of the Corsair had a taste of liver and heart. Because of the size of the crew, it was only a taste. As the liver of a game animal does not taste like liver of a beef cow, the crew were pleasantly surprised.

The next day, Pappy and I talked very politely with the cook, and he let us in the galley. We sliced the meat into small servings, and after putting flour on it, sauteed the meat on the grill. Then, placing the meat in a big iron pot, we covered it with cream of mushroom gravy. Now we let the meat simmer for about four hours.

That night the crew feasted on Swiss venison and mushroom gravy. The cook brought out some lobster tails as an additive. I mashed the potatoes and Pappy sliced some fresh pineapple for a salad. This gourmet dinner was washed down with plenty of home made red wine. The cook was smiling from ear to ear, and I knew we were eating like kings. So, let the wind blow. We were in snug harbor and life really was beautiful.

A Dive at Galapagos

Squinting my eyes against the bright, glaring light of the noontime sun, I looked ahead into the distant haze. There on the southern horizon was a gray speck. Shifting my elbows on the steel rail, I leaned over and looked down at the bow, knifing cleanly through the blue-green water. The foaming bow-wake danced and laughed in the never-ending race with our one hundred and forty-foot "Tuna Clipper." This fascinating spectacle had been my constant companion during the lonely eleven days since we left San Diego, California.

Looking up again at the speck on the horizon, I watched it slowly elongate into a thin, blue-gray line, Culpepper Island, northern most of the Archipelago de Colon. We were approaching those bleak, burnt, weather-scarred masses, that dotted the Pacific Ocean, six hundred miles off the coast of Ecuador, called the Galapagos Islands.

Millions of years ago, monumental volcanic upheavals had pushed masses of molten rock up from the ocean floor, to form the jagged, volcanic islands. Thousands of years of pounding seas had hollowed out caverns along their edges. Huge, jagged chunks of lava had been broken off, and pulled down into the unknown depths. For years the islands lay neglected, except for occasional sailing ships, stopping in for water and food. Then in the early part of the twentieth century, a fishing boat looking for tuna, found them in abundance among the northern most islands.

Not only was there tuna, but also great quantities of small fish necessary for baiting the tuna. Since then, the islands have become a favorite source of supply for Yellowfin Tuna. Part of the San Diego tuna fleet may be found there year around.

I pulled my rambling thoughts out of the distant haze, and back to the work at hand. My fishing gear was made up. I had enough poles, artificial lures, bait hooks and all the necessary equipment I might need. The bait receiver had been assembled early this morning, and the net was stacked in the big skiff, in

50

readiness for catching bait the next day.

Straightening up, and stretching, I took another look at the horizon, and started toward the galley on the main deck. Dropping down the ladder, I stood in the galley door, looking at the three golden apple pies the cook had just retrieved from the oven.

"Well, well, how's she going 'Cookie," I asked, as I reached for a cup, and eyed the fresh apple pies.

"Very good, kid. What's new on the bridge, and when we gonna get to the 'Rock'?"

I dropped a spoonful of sugar into the coffee I had just poured, and eased over to the pie.

"Looks like Culpepper coming up on the bow. If it is, we should be at the bait grounds in the morning, early."

I had a knife under a generous piece of pie, when the cook said, "Listen, kid, if ya eat that pie now, ya don't get none for ya dinner."

I didn't have to think it over, stay in good with the cook when you're at sea, and you'll `eat good' in most cases. In our case we ate well. The cook started washing some greens, and I kept one eye on the cooling apple pie.

The steady pounding of the engines seemed to die out a little, as if someone had closed the engine room door. I looked across the companion way into the engine room.

"What do ya say, fester-head? How's the coffee?" With that salutation the chief engineer, Walter Tucker, stepped into the galley. He was small, wiry and hard as nails, with a thin fringe of gray hair around the radar dome that was stuck on top of his shoulders.

"Good stuff, Chief," I said, as I held out my cup for a refill. "How's everything in the basement?"

"Everything's tickin'. How do your pumps work in the big skiff? Have you tried them out yet? Ya know, ya want to put a little of this cookin' oil in the check-valves. That's the best oil we've got for those springs."

"I got them all oiled up, Chief," I said from behind a cooling cup of coffee. "Jack and I overhauled them this morning when we mounted them."

The Chief took a large gulp of black coffee and said, "You know your divin' better than I do, but I can at least be sure the pumps are workin' OK before you boys go down. I don't want a pump going out while you boys are under the net. Then we'd take you home like fish, packed in ice." I heartily concurred.

The cook came over with his hands full of plates, and started setting the table for the evening meal. I washed out my cup, hung it up, and went topside to sit in the big skiff, and watch the evening sun go down. I always liked to see the evening sun go down. It meant the day's work was over, time for a little rest. Not only that, but it begins to get a little cooler. Most of the boys gather out on deck about sundown. They talk of the day's work, the women they know and what the people at home were doing.

The dark spot, in the gray haze on the horizon, had changed into an island off the starboard bow. I could make out the thousands of birds that live there, circling high in the air, in their never-ending search for food. Jack, who was my diving partner, was also our navigator. He was checking our position, and laying out the course for the night. The next morning, about daylight, we would be at the bait grounds.

The evening meal over, I sat out on deck in the big skiff, with my back against the net. The first evening stars were twinkling at us when Jack walked over, and dropped down beside me. He was tall, just a little more than six feet, had short curly hair and worked like a horse. I took the extended glass of red wine, and asked how our speed was holding up.

"We're making about thirteen knots," he said, as he made himself comfortable against the net. "We'll get to Elizabeth Bay tomorrow morning early, and it's going to be cold, too."

"Did the `Old Man' say where they're getting the salima?" Salima being a type of small bait found in the islands.

Jack idly scratched his knee, and looked around at me. "In the shallow water at Perry's Isthmus, from what I can hear on the

52

radio. At least the Skipper wanted to go there and start looking."

"That's not very deep," I said, "but there will be a lot of surge." We sipped on the red wine, looked at the stars, and talked about how we would work the net in the morning. On a `bait boat', getting the bait is always a problem. Catching bait along the coast of Central America was one thing, but apprehending those crafty little critters at Galapagos Islands was another. The skippers of most tuna boats catch live bait in Costa Rica, or Panama. Then they haul the bait to the Galapagos Islands. When the bait runs out, there is more live bait to be had in the Islands. There are various shallow places where salima are found.

Most of the time, the bait is in close to shore, in about two to six fathoms of water. The net fishes about six fathoms deep. This leaves some of the webbing, and the lead line, on the bottom. The bottom is made up of coral, lava, big and little rocks, with an occasional subterranean canyon running through it. Or maybe there is a ledge to drop off of, or a hole to fall into.

There are shimmering blue-white sandy patches where dog-face stingrays sleep, and spend their time. Sea urchins with five-inch spines cling to the smooth rocks. Moray eels, and lobsters, hide in the darker shadows, while thousands of multicolored tropical fish dart from one rock to another. Once in a while a giant manta ray glides by, and it's a happy day when the diver doesn't see a big shark. Your heart pounds because you know that it would only take a second for a big one to tear your arm off. You're in fifty-five degree waters, but still the clammy perspiration breaks out on your face.

The net must be closed, so you work on, regardless of the sharks. If a shark is less than six feet in length, we disregard it. When they are eight or ten-foot long, we watch them a little closer.

There are Whitetip, Mako, Blue Nose, Tiger, and maybe Great White sharks. In the early days at Galapagos, we didn't know about the Great White. Off Albemarle reef, on the northern end of Isabela Island, there are huge sharks. In a frenzy of hate, they would attack a fishing boat. I have watched them bite the steel racks, and try to bite the guard rail on the boat.

Under these conditions the diver works. The equipment, consisting of only a seventy-five-pound helmet, is good to a depth of forty feet. To go deeper than that, is not advisable. The divers gather up an armful of webbing, and lead line, then back up, pulling the rest of the webbing along. When the bottom of the net is together, it is sent up to be stacked in the big skiff. By this time the sharks and rays are on the outside, and the live bait is on the inside. The diver comes up, freezing cold, gasping for air, but feeling the job was well done. His pay, maybe a shot of whiskey, a cigarette, a pat on the back, then he sits and freezes for a while. He is so cold he can't speak, his lips are blue and sometimes he is sick to his stomach, and throwing up his last meal. But just leave him alone for a few minutes, and he'll be all right.

That's what diving at Galapagos is like. Sometimes you get waters with lots of rays, but no sharks, next time you get sharks but no rays. Then you turn around, and find yourself in deep water, screaming to release the pressure on your ears. You come up, blood running out of your nose, asking why the net had been dropped in that depth of water. After making dive after dive, with the same partner, you get to respect him, especially after he has pulled you out of a few tight spots.

We were up the next morning bright and early, had breakfast, put the gear in the water, and were rubbing tobacco on the face-plate of the diving helmet, when the sun came up over Isabela Island. We skirted along the shore-line of Isabela Island, at Perry's Isthmus. Most of us were in the big skiff, with the little skiff bobbing along behind us. Harold Morgan, our skipper, was also our `bait man.' He stood on the bow of the work-boat, which was towing both the big and little skiffs. Harold was pure bone and muscle, and those two hundred and some odd pounds were stacked up to about six-feet-two. He had eyes that could look down into the murky depths, and find bait when the rest of us couldn't see bottom in one fathom.

Jack worked beside me as we rubbed the face plates of the helmets with a cigarette, both inside and out. The tobacco cleans, and puts a film on the glass face plate. We set our helmets on the starboard side of the big skiff, saw the hundred feet of air hose attached to the helmet was coiled down like we wanted it. We looked at the hand-operated pumps, which sent down the life-giving air and sat down on the thwart.

"Well, buddy, here we are again," I said, as I stuffed two sticks of gum into my mouth.

"Ya," he said in a serious, confidential whisper. "Some day I'm gonna take an oar, and walk toward Texas. When I got to a place where someone asks me what that thing is, I'm gonna stop and build myself a house. I'm gonna live there, and never look at the ocean again."

That was what we had told each other for more than three years. We'll never do it. We don't know any other trade. Besides, the ocean gets in your blood.

The engine of the speedboat sputtered, and slowed down. "Take a look down there, and see what size bait that is," Harold said, as he pointed the direction he wanted the boat to go.

Behind me, one of the crew dropped the glass-bottom box over the side, and into the cool morning water. Holding it against the motion of the water, he peered down into the shadowy depths below.

"It looks like medium salima, Harold. Balled up pretty good, too," his voice, somewhat muffled, echoed from the glass bottomed looking box.

Harold looked back at us, "What'd he say?" There seemed to be a note of irritation in Harold's voice.

"Salima, balled up." I yelled back at him.

Harold was all business now. It was his job to set the net around the salima. After the net was set, it was Jack's and my job to go down, and bring the lead line together, which is the bottom of the net. Then, when we had the bottom of the net together, one of us would send it up, and the other would clear snags along the rocky bottom.

We had almost completed the second circle around the bait, when Harold yelled back, "Let 'er go." That's all it took. I pulled the toggle pin holding the bow line of the little skiff. The little skiff turned sideways, and pulled against the end of the net. The net ran out as Jack and I pulled on our cotton gloves. Halfway around, we dumped the `sack' and continued the circle to pick up the little skiff, with the opposite end of the net in it.

A heaving line came across from the little skiff. The other men were pulling in the heaving line, with the end of the net in tow, as I slipped over the side, into the cool morning water. I hung chest deep in the chilly water, waiting for the helmet. The seventy-five pounds of hand-pounded copper, which was the diving helmet, was placed over my head, and came to rest on my shoulders. With my left hand I pulled the air hose in after me, wound it around my left shoulder once, and heard a hand slap twice on the outside of my helmet. I had one end of the net in my right hand, and the other end in my left. Slowly, I lowered myself down into the world of limped lights, and murky shadows. Gone was the sun that had peaked at us from over Isabella Island. Gone were the voices of my shipmates. The other world, in which men live, had vanished. I lowered myself hand under hand into the fascinating world of fish, pulling the net together as I descended.

I kept going down and down, with only the gentle, soft shoo-shoo of the air, as it hissed into my helmet. The pressure that built up in my ears I relieved, by chewing gum and yelling. My ears popped and I kept going down. As I descended, I continued to pull the ends of the net together, working from the inside of the net.

I hit bottom in about five fathoms. I looked off into the shadows, looked like the bottom was going to be good. It was a lava flow, which had broken off, mostly flat, with a few jagged rocks sticking up here and there. Turning to my left, I saw Jack had landed and was looking at me. He looked big in the shimmering stillness of the frosty water, because objects seen through this type of face plate are magnified and distorted.

With the lead line in my hands, I leaned over and started to work myself along the left wing of the net. Jack would be working along the right wing, and we should meet near the center of the net. After that we would work back along the wing, pulling the bottom of the net toward each other, until we finally arrived below the big skiff. This procedure is followed repeatedly, until the bottom of the net is overlapping, and sometimes tied securely with small pieces of twine.

Starting the second phase of this operation, I worked my way along the bottom of the net, until I came to the first snag. Most of the time it is easier to kick a snag loose with your foot, because your arms are usually full of webbing. I could tell by the amount of webbing left on the bottom that I was working in about six fathoms.

The sack, which was our halfway mark, loomed up before me. I looked for Jack, but couldn't see him. So I worked on along his wing. I could feel him pulling against the lead line, so I knew I was near him.

With an abruptness that made my heart skip a beat, a seal put its nose against the face plate, and glared in at me. It is a strange feeling to glance up, and look into a pair of big brown eyes, only inches from your face. I wondered why the eyes are always brown. Are there any blue-eyed seals? Seals won't hurt you, at least that is what I have been told. I have never been bitten by one, and hope I never am, they have teeth similar to a big police dog. The seal disappeared as he had arrived, in a swirl of water, and I was left looking off into the blue-green mist at a dark object.

As I worked on toward it, I saw bubbles coming up from the other side. Jack had arrived at a large rock, and was having a tough time trying to get the net over it. We were both under the webbing now. If we lost our helmets, we would be caught like a fish in a net. When you are on the surface, you think about these times, and hate them. But someone has to do the job, so you shrug your shoulders, and go down again.

I worked up to the rock gathering the webbing and the lead line as I went. I could still feel Jack pulling, and kicking at the lead line, on the far side of the rock. Gathering up the webbing, I lifted it up as high as I could. I took a breath and ducked under the webbing. Now I was on the outside of the net. Pulling my air hose after me, I worked along the edge of the rock, and there was Jack, pushing against the net, trying to get between the net and the rock, so he could clear the lead line.

It is strange how two people working together know what the other person is thinking. Jack knew what I was thinking, so he climbed up on top of the rock and started to pull the webbing up. He picked it up as I pulled it out from the bottom. It works well that way, when you have a large rock to get over.

Jack dropped down on the other side with the webbing. I was on the outside of the net, kicking out the snags with my feet, while Jack pulled the lead line, and webbing, into him. I could just make him out in the distant shadows. A dark object came down, stopped by my helmet for a moment, then disappeared back into the shadows. No doubt my friend, the seal.

We worked our way back to the sack, and Jack went on down the left wing. I gathered up the webbing, ducked under it, and came up on the inside of the net. Well, if Jack is on the other wing, I'll work this side, I thought. It didn't make any difference.

I worked from the sack back to a spot just below the skiff. There were two little sharks outside the net, looking for salima to get caught in the webbing. Then the sharks would work up to the salima and bite at them. When we saw small sharks doing that we would kick at them. As far as I was concerned, the big ones could eat the salima, and the net too, if they wanted it badly enough. I was working with an arm load of webbing, about halfway between the skiff and the sack, when I stepped off into space. As I started to fall, my knee hit a sharp outcropping of lava. I saw the ledge I had been standing on go by my face plate. I was kicking and trying to swim at the same time.

My hand fell on a pinnacle of rock and I held on. My feet

kicked out several small rocks, before I got a footing, and started to haul myself back up on the ledge. I made the ledge, breathed deeply and stood there. Looking down I could see what appeared to be white sand, about three fathoms on down. I shuddered slightly, from the cold, grabbed the led line and started to pull the webbing up to the edge of the drop-off. As I did this, I tried to picture what we had around us, the structure of the bottom at that particular point. I had worked up to the other wing with good bottom all the way, this wing had good bottom also, therefore, we must have set the net around a short canyon in the ocean floor. It might have been some type of a little blowhole, formed at the same time the islands were. This promised another problem. The net would have to be pulled across it.

Working along the edge of the subterranean cliff, I realized that not only was the water very cold, but something was wrong with the air pump. Instead of the steady rhythm of the plungers pressing the air down to me, there was a break, which left me gasping for breath. One of the plungers was missing, so I was only getting half of the oxygen I had been receiving before.

To work at a given speed, you have to use a given amount of oxygen, and if you only get half the oxygen, you only work at half the speed. In most cases, when a diver received only half the amount that he should be getting, he will return to the surface, but the net was almost closed. I decided to stay down, and finish the job.

I gathered up another arm load of webbing, and slowly backed to the edge of the cliff. In this method I worked my way along the edge, gasping for air at every step. About fifteen feet along the cliff's edge, I came to a small outcropping of coral heads and rock. I lifted the lead line over the main body of coral, and started back toward the edge. In front of me I could see several rocks caught in the net. As the rocks were small, I pulled with all my strength, and stepped back. Step followed step, and pull followed pull, until with a sudden twist and turn, the rocks beneath my feet gave away, and I knew I was falling into liquid space. I gasped a breath of air, my hands clawed at the sharp lava rocks as I went down, but they came loose with my weight.

The seventy-five-pound helmet was turning me over sideways. Through the face plate I saw the side of the cliff go by, and then the helmet filled with water. Upside down in the midst of falling lava, rocks and coral heads, I landed on the bottom with the debris of an underwater landslide slowly settling on me. Holding my breath, and my eyes open, I felt for the sandy bottom, found it and knew I was on my back, half buried in rock and coral. Bubbles from the back of my helmet shot past my head, and pushed the water out of the upper part of the helmet, leaving my face once again in air, so I could breathe.

Slowly I began to breathe again, my heart pounding in my throat. My body was numb from the cold, and I was pinned by my legs under the rock slide. The equipment is built for six fathoms, not ten. But here I lay, with my head splitting. The pressure on my ears felt like someone was driving ice picks into them. I tried to reach for the rocks that held me, but couldn't. I then realized that I was trapped in ten fathoms of water. The cliff rose up beside me and beyond that — cold, blue-green water. As long as the air came down to me, I would be all right, but if it stopped for any reason, I would quite simply drown. A small fish stopped, looked in at me, and swam on. I saw the bottom of the net drop over the edge of the cliff above me, and hang there. I knew, as it slowly began to move, that the men up above were pulling it in. I tried to relax so my heart wouldn't pound so. My lungs ached from the lack of oxygen, and there I waited.

The net disappeared completely, and I knew it wouldn't be long now. Buried under sixty feet of water, I peered out of the face plate, of what well might be my coffin.

After what seemed like hours, but in reality was only a few minutes, there was a faint pull on my helmet. I reached up and grabbed the air hose with both hands, and pulled twice. This is the signal to pull up. I felt a long pull, but not enough to pull me out of the rock slide, so I continued to wait. The minutes dragged on, then I could feel a quick steady pull on the air hose. Then a hand touched my shoulder, and I looked into the face plate of my diving partner, Jack R. Vore. With a twisted leer, and blood running from his nose, Jack went to work on the rocks that held me. I felt him pull on my left leg. It came loose. Then my right was out. He tried to lift me up. Then he helped me wrap the air hose around my chest, and pulled on it twice. Slowly I felt myself being lifted off the bottom, and gently drift upwards. The pressure changed, my ears crackled like fire crackers, and then my helmet bumped against the big skiff. I tried to help them as they reached down to pull me aboard, and lay me on the net. I was freezing cold, and shaking uncontrollably, as I gulped down great quantities of air. But, believe me, I was never so glad to see the sunshine in all my life.

So now, I turn my head a little when my friends talk to me. My left ear isn't what it used to be. When the sun goes down, and the evening meal is over, you'll still find us in the big skiff. We are still drinking home-made red wine, and telling sea stories. The stories get around to the world below —- that world of shimmering, blue-green water, and I find myself once again telling about the subterranean land slide, and good old Jack pulling me out.

M. V. Chicken of the Sea with airplane on canopy.

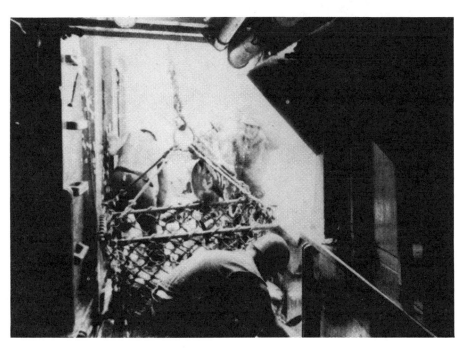

John Princeiapto, Ben Crobarger at brail on Sun Pacific.
Tony Tavares is Captain.

Bob Rood with lobsters caught off La Jolla.

Fishing 2 pole tuna on the Atlantic. Capt. Manuel Matis
Bud Maricle corner rack. John Silva & John Gnomes fish.

Bait Receiver with Joe Rosa – Gem of the Sea.

Bait Receiver with Vern Bowman – American Beauty.

M. V. American Beauty – Vern Bowman Captain.

Fernandina Is. Galapagos – seen from Elizabeth Bay.

Chicken of the Sea – out 3 months with full load.

Arch at Culpepper Is. Northern most of Galapagos.

Red Crone, Armon Tavares & Others on Sun Pacific.

Red Crone, Armon Tavares & Others on Sun Pacific.

Julio Guidi, Frank Tarantino, Louie Guidi, and Marco.
Four pole on the tuna boat Lou Jean.

3 Pole – Chicken of the Sea. Ed Suman under tuna.

Redondo Rock. Galapagos Islands.

4 Pole on the Lou Jean, Patria in back. Socorro Island.

Heavy 2 Pole. Chicken of the Sea. Harold Morgan Capt.

Modern picture of Puntarenas, C.R. – Pier at right.

The Great Anchor Drop

We took departure from Galera Point, Ecuador, and were bound for Panama Canal with a full load of bananas. For several years, we had been running from Galveston, Texas south to Panama. Passing southbound through the Canal, we would proceed to Guayaquil, Ecuador, load a cargo of fruit, then head back north for Panama. We'd transit the Canal northbound, and then on to Galveston. By now we had local knowledge, like natives.

On this northbound trip, we were starting into the shipping lanes about thirty miles south of Tobaguilla Island, Panama. We were watching for traffic in and out of Panama. It was my watch, but John Radine, the Captain, couldn't sleep and he was on the bridge, too. I got us both a cup of coffee, and we sat on the bridge talking; it was 0400. Going out on the port wing of the bridge, I set up the pelorus for a 45-degree angle. We would be up to the Taboga light soon.

I told Captain John I was going forward, and would get the anchor ready to drop. Although we were still several hours off, my attitude was to be ready. John said, "Okay, but tell one of the seamen to do it."

"If I do it, I know everything is right," I replied. This started a lecture. By the time John stopped talking, I could have cleared the anchor.

John turned to me and said, "Listen, you've been doing this all the time. You tell the crew to get the anchor ready. Now that's an order."

I turned to Ortega and Mite, two Ecuadorian seamen, and gave the order. They said, "Si, Piloto," and were gone.

I waited fifteen minutes or so, and they didn't return to the bridge. I told Capt. John I was going forward to have a look. I went forward and down one deck to the room with the anchor capstans. There they were, trying to do something, God knows what. They had chipped off the concrete from the haws pipe, where the chain ran out, but the "dog," or "keeper" was still in place.

I took a five-foot bar, stuck it in the handle for the brake, and pulled hard. The brake was tight. I then took a sledge hammer, and knocked the keeper out, clearing the chain to run out.

Well, it did! Making 16 knots, in 40 fathoms of water, and in the shipping lanes, I had just dropped the starboard anchor. Clawing my way up the ladder, I ran down the deck, yelling to John, "Back her down, back her down! I just dropped the starboard anchor!"

At this point let me explain something. This ship is diesel electric, with pilot house control. When we were out to sea, all of the ship's power is generated by the ship's main engines. The engineers, as yet, had not changed the ship's electric power over to an auxiliary engine. When John backed down, all of the ship's power was cut off. That meant no steering, no radio, no lights, and the ice machines kicked out. The refrigeration system flooded with Freon 22, the refrigerant.

The men in the engine room were frantically starting engines, throwing switches, and using foul language in general. A super-tanker went by calling us with its blinker light. The Captain sat in his big chair, looking out the window.

In a short time, we had electric power back on line. I started hauling in the anchor. There were two seamen in the chain locker, the next deck down, to flake out the anchor chain. There are nine shots to a chain, and fifteen fathoms to a shot. With six feet to a fathom, we had out about 135 fathoms of chain, or 810 feet.

As the anchor chain rumbled around the capstan, I inspected the brake band. The brake band was placed underneath, where it was out of sight. I finally found that the brake, instead of being tight, was loose, or off. The seamen had turned the brake handle the wrong way, and had tightened it with a bar. When I checked to see if the brake was on, it was really off. Therefore, the anchor had dropped.

It was daylight when I finally set the anchor. The ship vibrated and came to life, once again we were underway. We were late for our scheduled "lock-up" in the canal. The pilot wanted to know where we were. Some ship made a complaint by radio to the shipping department in Panama about a ship with no running lights. They in turn, called the pilot station. Now the pilot was talking with the Captain.

In the thirteen hours it took to transit the canal, the Captain and the pilot chatted away. I sat on a stool, like a dunce, and steered the ship. The only time the pilot talked to me was when he gave a command for the ship's movement, which was seldom. We cleared Panama Canal, headed into the Caribbean, and I set a course for San Andres Island. The ship's clock rang two bells, 0100. I had been on the bridge for twenty-two hours straight.

I found peace and quiet in my room. Stretching out in my bunk, I thought about the . . . but was fast asleep in the arms of Morpheus.

I sat down to breakfast with the chief engineer across from me. He just looked at me, not a word. The Captain did say, "Good morning," but nothing else. The refrigeration engineer didn't even smile. Finishing my bacon and eggs and another cup of coffee, I went up to the bridge. Even the seaman on watch just silently picked up the binoculars and look at the distant horizon.

This trip northbound to Galveston was very pleasant. Not a soul talked to me. By the time we were a day out of Galveston, the seamen were talking to me and the Captain was smiling again. I have never heard of a man dropping the anchor from a ship moving at full speed in the shipping lanes, and in shallow soundings. Believe me, when you do this, you have the attention of the entire crew and a few people ashore. You do not make friends with Captains, either.

Revolution in Ecuador

The Atlantic Reefer was anchored just off the Molicone in the Guayas River, Ecuador. Our cargo was not ready, and the lights of Guayaquil beckoned, so I cleaned up and went ashore. The captain, John Radine, was already ashore, the watch was set, and so I thought, why not?

I was first officer on the Reefer, and we hauled bananas from South America up to the States. We had worked out of Guayaquil for about two years, so we knew a lot of people here. As we made a trip about every 22 days, we were known to bring in various items from the States. Two of our very good friends were Fred and Nada David, who ran the Majestic Hotel.

Nada was a fiery, redheaded music teacher, while Fred was a Hungarian-born world-traveling linguist. Fred spoke seventeen languages fluently. Because of his past experience, Fred now managed the Majestic Hotel for the Brazonie brothers. Often, when the Reefer was in Guayaquil and not loading cargo, I could be found in the Majestic.

As I walked up Nuevo de Octobre, the main drag in Guayaquil, I noticed the army on every corner. They were setting up sandbags and some tanks were rumbling around, so I just whistled and walked on up the street. Then in the distance I heard a few random shots, small arms fire.

The Majestic was about five blocks up and one block to the right. As I rounded the corner, I stepped over some sandbags, where two solders were setting up a machine gun. They just looked at me. I gave them a big smile and said, "Good afternoon" in my best Spanish. I walked on, but kept thinking of a seaman on the Scarlet Queen who had been shot in the back. That was in Managua, and he was just walking away, too.

I heard one shot somewhere as I was stepping through the door into the Majestic. Fred was standing by the door with some other people. We shook hands, and Fred asked if I had heard the news.

I countered with, "How could I?"

The story was that some students, in one of the colleges Ecuador has, had started a revolution. The army had moved in immediately and set up roadblocks. Only the army was on the street, all others must stay inside. There would not be any cargo loaded until the army moved out.

Captain Radine had a room for two, so I picked up a key from Fred and went up to the third floor. Giving a knock on the wood door, I entered the room and there was John reading a newspaper. Walking over to the window, I peered out. The army was all over the street. Stretching out on the piece of wood they call a bed, I asked John what the paper had to say.

John said the college students were marching around in Quito, the capital, and some army officers had joined them. This was a show of force by the regular army. As long as we were inside there would be no trouble. Maybe in a few days this would end, and we could load bananas.

In about the year 1522, Francisco Pizarro, a poorly educated, illegitimate conquistador, invaded Ecuador. Although this army moved by boat along the coast, later they moved into the mountains. Francisco's half-brother, Gonzalo Pizarro, is the one who was governor of Quito in 1539. Then in 1541, Gonzalo led the expedition east into the Amazon Basin.

Because Ecuador is about 70% bush-indian, and by tradition the conquering army came from the mountains, the people in the lowland hate the people in the highlands. There are small army garrisons along the coast, but the command is from the mountains. So even today, 400 years after Pizarro, there is hatred between the two areas. This is why the army was in Guayaquil.

John and I stayed in our room until dinner time, then walked down one floor to the dining room. We sat at a long, well decorated table with about fifteen other guests of the Majestic. These people were from all over the world, and about five languages were being spoken. English, Spanish and German were predominate. As the owners of the Majestic were Italian that language was also spoken.

The food was served European style, with plenty of red and white wine. The small talk ranged from China to Germany. Everyone would speak in German, then someone would change to Italian. In a few minutes we were all speaking in English. After the meal was over, which took about two hours, the table was cleared and we began talking about the revolution. Most of these men were merchants, selling goods from all over the world. As long as the army was here, none of them could leave.

The next morning, we were up at daylight and down in the dining room. Breakfast for them is a cup of hot milk, with coffee essence, and a sourdough biscuit. Americans live a different life style, and John and I were not about to change. We called Fred over and asked him for bacon and eggs. The bacon was obtainable, but the eggs had to be scrambled. The eggs are brought in from the foothills on horseback. They are placed in small sacks, which in turn are placed in larger sacks. The end product results in most of the eggs being broken. We ate our breakfast and, to the amazement of the mess boy, washed it down with large cups of black coffee.

During the day there were some fights in the street. I heard a few shots fired, and the army tanks drove up and down the blocks. All of the people stayed in the Majestic, now and then looking out. Most of us sat around the long table in the dining room talking of the various countries and how the world had changed after World War II.

The next day we were up early and looking out the window. We watched the tanks go by. Army trucks were moving up and down the street, picking up the machine-guns and sandbags. The two-day student uprising was over. There had been several people killed, and a lot of people jailed. In all reality, we were just onlookers; now we could go to work.

Capt. Radine and I walked the six blocks to the Molicone and took a launch out to the Reefer. The ship's broker, Colonel Alban Borja came aboard to arrange the loading of the fruit, and we were back to normal.

As the current in the Guayas River runs from six to eight knots, the ships have to anchor in the river. Lighters are brought alongside loaded with green bananas, and planks are placed from a lighter to the loading port. The cargo holds are prechilled to about 60 degrees, and the fruit comes aboard at outside temperature. The longshoremen carry one stem, which weighs about 100 pounds, up the plank. This goes on day and night until the ship is loaded.

About every four months we would have a man fall overboard. If the man could not make his way to shore, then he drowned. There was no effort made to save him. Human life was worth nothing here.

With a full load of fruit and the pilot aboard, we hoisted the anchor. We maneuvered the ship around and headed down the twenty-nine miles of river. Dropping the pilot and guards off at the Puna Pilot Station, the ship was now bound for the open ocean. Captain Radine and I sat in our big, leather-covered chairs on the bridge and drank coffee. Once again we had seen a small uprising in a strange country. I set a course for Panama, and thought how good it was to be an American. I watched the evening sun go down in the west, and I knew it was not only good, but it was great to be an American.

Over the Side With Him

The M. V. Atlantic Reefer was moored dockside in Balboa, Panama, C. Z. We were a refrigerated cargo ship running from the United States to South America. We would deliver general cargo southbound, and bananas northbound. About every twenty- two days we would transit the Panama Canal, once northbound and once southbound. Over the years that we were on this run, we became friendly with a lot of people. One of these friends was the ship's broker.

On this trip northbound through the Canal, the Captain came to me and said he had a new man for the crew. Our crew was mostly Ecuadoreans, who worked with the bananas and lived in Guayaquil. When I met this new seaman, and signed him on the ship's crew list, I found he was a Latvian. He looked like any other American seaman, tanned and well-built. The ship's broker had spoken to the Captain, and the Captain, not being up on his world history, hired the man for the crew. Now the Latvian was a member of the ship's crew, and we were headed north.

With all of the fighting in Europe, with Germany and Russia, with the breaking up of small countries, the Baltic countries of Lithuania, Latvia and Estonia no longer existed. This generated a great many men without a country. They had no home, and could not be put ashore on any land. If they returned home, they would be killed.

To get rid of this Latvian, who was held by the ship's broker, our Captain had made him one of our crew. Now we had this man on board who could not be put ashore, and he could not be fired. The Latvian knew we could not discharge him. He had seaman's papers, but no country to send him home to. So the Latvian would lay out on deck and sleep. He would not work. I could not discharge him, and I did not wish to use violence to make him work. I had a problem.

Several months went by, and we made our run back and forth to Ecuador. Several men in the crew asked me if I would like the

69

Latvian to vanish from the face of the earth. There is no problem doing this in these ports. As the ship was under Liberian Registry, we came under Liberian law. Liberia did not have a Maritime Counsel; therefore, they could not make a law. There was no country to inquire into the disappearance of a person. I told these man not to kill him. I would think of something else. We had several fights on board, in which I intervened. Then one night while I was on watch, I had the answer.

We took a cargo out of Ecuador, made the Canal transit north bound, and were one day out of Galveston, Texas. I called four of the crew up to the bow where we could not be overheard, and laid out my plan. The men laughed loud and long. They thought the plan was great, and said to count them in. I cautioned them not to say a word, or all would be lost. Above all, do not let the Captain know.

The Atlantic Reefer pulled up to the outer sea buoy at Galveston, The pilot came aboard, and we started up the channel. We made a left turn and tied up at Pier 22. As we off-loaded the cargo, we took on supplies, and by sundown the next day were ready for sea. The pilot came aboard, we cleared Pier 22 and headed into the channel.

While the Captain talked with the pilot, I walked out on the starboard wing of the bridge. I looked aft, and there were the crewmen leaning against the railing. They had the Latvian with them, and were pointing to the hotels along the shoreline. I looked forward to the pilot boat, waiting for us at the outer sea buoy. Then I slowed the ship to half-speed.

As we came up to the outer sea buoy, I stopped the main engine. The pilot shook hands with the Captain and then with me, and wished us a pleasant voyage. The pilot boat came along the port side, where our boarding ladder had been placed. The Captain waved goodby to the pilot, and then went below to his room. I looked to see that the propeller was not turning over, and then stepped out on the starboard wing.

I thought of the months the Latvian had been aboard; of the

months he would not work. Looking aft at the crew surrounding the Latvian, I gave the signal. With a smile on my lips, I'll never forget watching the crew throw that man overboard. The Latvian sailed off the boat deck, turning over several times before hitting the water. I watched to see if he was clear, and then started the main engine. The pilot boat started blowing its whistle.

The ship was now past the outer sea buoy, and came under the law of the high seas. No longer were we governed by the law of United States, and Liberia has no law. I rang the engine room to set the governors on the engines; we were now full speed ahead. As the Captain came up to the bridge, I walked out on the wing.

The little pilot boat was still blowing her whistle, as she picked up the Latvian. The Captain stood beside me, looking aft at the pilot boat. After a short pause he turned to me and asked what happened.

I grinned from ear to ear, and said, "I think the Latvian fell overboard." The four crewmen were on the bridge as the Captain broke out a bottle of Scotch whiskey.

The Captain had to bring out another bottle when the rest of the crew came through. There wasn't room enough on the bridge. We all agreed the job was well done. The crew went below, the watch was set, and I sat down in my big, overstuffed chair. One of the seamen brought me a cup of coffee, as I put my feet up on the engine room telegraph. There was quiet about the decks, and I talked to the evening watch about the Latvian. As I sat in the big chair and drank my coffee, I thought of how in a blink of an eye, that Latvian became an airborne missile. How with a wave of the hand, he was over the side.

Aground in the Jambeli River

We were headed south off the coast of Ecuador. Passing Santa Elena Point on our port hand, we swung south-southeast toward the mouth of the Jambeli River. At 2100 hours, we crossed the Gulf of Guayaquil, with Puna Island on our port hand. Captain John Radine was out on the starboard wing of the bridge, while I was master-minding the dim lights in the pilot-house. There were two Puna Island Indians in the pilot-house with me.

As this ship was diesel-electric, and pilot-house control, all arrangements had been made for maneuvering. The Jambeli River drains the banana country in the southern tip of Ecuador, and once again we would load fruit from this river. Our job was to take the ship, M. V. Atlantic Reefer, up the Jambeli River about four miles, and anchor off of Puerto Bolivar. The fruit was brought to us in lighters, and came from Machalla, Santa Rosa, and the surrounding area.

Capt. Radine and I had navigated in this river many times in the past, and were well aware of the mud flats, sand bars, and shallow soundings. The night was black, with a light rain, as we approached the mouth of the river. I called to John and asked if he wanted the radar turned on. He answered in the negative, so I just turned on the fathometer. I took the ship off auto-pilot, and had one of the Indians start steering by hand. The ship was going at half-speed, but I could only see one light through the rain.

As ships head into the Jambeli River, there are two lighted buoys on the left. With Jambeli Island on the right, we should be in three fathoms of water at the first buoy. We were now in three fathoms of water under the keel.

The rain picked up a little, and John mumbled something about the weather as I looked at the fathometer — three fathoms! I could only see one faint light, far ahead, just to the left. Calling to John, and stopping the main engine at the same time, I told him we were in three fathoms now. John yelled back to go ahead, we would anchor by the distant light.

By now, the two Puna Indians were hopping up and down. One of them came over to me and, pointing out the starboard door, said we were now in the river. The night was dark, but the black we were observing was Jambeli Island. The Indians were right.

At that moment Capt. Radine stepped into the pilot house. "We are in the river. Hard left, and slow ahead. Let's go out on a reciprocal course." Reciprocal means to change course 180 degrees.

The problem was, the first light was out, and we were almost to the second light. Now I turned on the radar. I could see the land mass, and also the two buoys, then the ship stopped turning. I looked at the compass, stopped the main engine, and told John we were aground. The rain poured down, and John said a lot of very foul words in three or four languages, ending with ". . . check the tide tables." These rivers do have ocean tides, and a high tide would be at 0300. I checked the water depth at the bow and stern, we were eight feet into the mud, at the bow.

Capt. Radine, the Chief Engineer, and I were in the galley by 0245. John told the Chief he wanted full power on the main generators, which supplied power to the main drive motor. The Chief said fine, he would wire the governors up, and we would have maximum power.

I finished my coffee and went to the bridge with John. The ship was alive. You could feel the vibration of the big main engines.

John turned to me and said, "When we go astern, I want you to swing the rudder from hard-over too hard-over."

"But John, that's not good seamanship. Never go hard-over when you're full astern," I said as I looked at the ship's clock. John looked at me and said, "I want to throw the water up each side of the bow to wash out the mud. I want to break the suction."

As the clock struck six bells, John put the ship full astern, then stepped out on the starboard wing. I washed the rudder hard left and then hard right. About the forth time the rudder was hard-over, the ship came free of the mud bank. There was a bumping sound, somewhere deep down below. I stopped the main engine. We were clear of the mud, and John said, "Hard right, and slow ahead."

The rudder angle indicator was hard right, and I put the ship slow ahead. There was no response from the rudder. We did not turn right. I stopped the main engine, turned to my right and marched out on the wing to tell John we had just lost the rudder. In the driving rain I heard expletives that are seldom used anymore, even by marines, both in English, Yugoslavian, and Spanish. I did pick out, ". . . drop the anchor." I went forward and dropped the anchor.

As daylight broke and the rain eased up, we were anchored in the center of the Jambeli River, Ecuador. The pilot boat from Puerto Bolivar, the town on the river, brought out all of the officials. They sat around the big table in the galley, and everyone talked at once.

In the end, one of the plantation owners said he had a light airplane, and would fly John to Guayaquil. There were no telephones in Puerto Bolivar. John flew to Guayaquil, and called the owners in San Diego.

Five hours later the pilot boat came out, with John on it, wearing the longest face I have ever seen. John had explained to the owners what had happened. In the end, the owners told John, that as we had caused this trouble, we could fix this trouble.

We ate lunch, and formed a plan. First we had to find out if the entire rudder was gone, or just part. Was the rudder post sheared off, or were the rudder post and flange all right? To find this out, someone had to dive down under the ship and look. I seemed to be the most logical person.

We tied several life preservers on a long line, and let them drift a long way off of the stern. We rigged a wooden ladder over the side, and then ran a line all the way under the ship. This line was tied to the railing on one side of the ship, and then led under the ship and up to the railing on the other side. The river water was muddy, so I could not see anything.

I would have to feel the rudder post, and in my mind remember how it was put together. If I lost my hold, I would come up going down river. We didn't have any type of diving gear, so this dive would be holding my breath, and hope for the best. There was one other problem; this water was part salt water and part fresh water. When a shark is in this type of water, he may become vicious. These shores do have big sharks, so this was on my mind. I lowered myself into the muddy water.

I held onto the keel rope, then with a deep breath, I pulled myself down under the ship. The rudder post was about sixteen feet down. I opened my eyes, but that was useless. Visibility was zero, or one foot at best. I could feel the rudder post, and on the end was the large flange. Beneath this flange there was only space. I held onto the flange with one arm and waved my other arm below the flange. There was no question. The rudder was gone.

I let go, and the river current carried me down stream. I pulled for the surface as hard as I could. Breaking the surface of the water, I grabbed the line with the life preservers tied on the end. Up on deck the crew were yelling, and pulling me in. I felt like a piece of live bait, on the end of a fishing line. All I could think of was, I hoped the shark fishing is bad.

John met me with a bottle of Scotch whiskey, and he even had ice. We sat on deck and looked at the jungle, the muddy river, and drank a good scotch. I explained to him what I had found, confirming our thoughts. At this time, we made the decision to take the ship to Guayaquil, and beach it there. We would have to beach it several times, to create a new rudder.

The next morning we had a pilot and two little tugboats along side. We timed our departure so we could go up the Guayas River on the flood tide. We pulled the anchor, and the little remolcas huffed and puffed along the side. When we turned our main propulsion motor over, there was a heavy vibration in the ship. We then knew something was wrong with the propeller. The rudder had gone through the propeller, and it was bent or broken.

We crossed the Jambeli Canal and headed up the Guayas River. By sundown we were anchored off the Molicone, at Guayaquil. The two little tugboats stayed with us, for we would need them in the future. In the end, we beached the ship seven times. We were there six weeks, but that is another story.

Capt. Radine and I cleaned up, set the watch, and went ashore. In the warm evening, we walked up the streets of Guayaquil, and went into the Majestic Hotel. Fred and Nada, good friends of ours, were the managers and part owners. We sat at the long table, in the dinning room on the second floor, and stirred the ice in our drinks. How could two people get into so much trouble so easily? This time we had managed to run the Atlantic Reefer aground in the Jambeli River.

Building a New Rudder

The M.V. Atlantic Reefer had run aground entering the Jambeli River, in the southern part of Ecuador. After Captain John Radine had talked by telephone to the owner, Anton Martinolich, in San Diego, our job was to build a new rudder.

Starting down the Jambeli River with two little tugboats, or remolcas as they are called, we soon found the propeller had also been damaged. Although the propeller had sustained some damage, we established that we could still turn it over slowly, which helped the remolcas a great deal.

With a pilot, and some plantation owners, on board for the ride, we headed north, across the Jambeli Canal. Arriving off Puna Island, we entered the Guayas River. Winding our way up the thirty miles of river to Guayaquil, we dropped anchor off the Molicone. Because this river will run as much as eight knots, depending on the rain, we let out fifteen fathoms of anchor chain. The anchor chain will stretch out, and the water hyoscine will float down the river and foul up on the chain.

The next morning John and I went ashore, hailed a taxi, and went over the hill to a small boat repair yard. The ship carpenters had never built a rudder that large, but they said they could do the job. We would have to draw a plan, with all of the dimensions, and present it to them. As there are sixteen hardwoods in South America, Lignum Vitae was selected because of the availability.

With a plan in hand, John and I returned to the boat works. We explained the what and why, and the job was started. A crew was sent into the jungle to fell a Lignum Vitae tree. The wood was then shaped into pieces ten inches square by eight feet long. These, in turn, were banded together and secured with iron bands. Pinning the wood with iron pins from band to band, a new rudder was fashioned.

Our next problem was to find a place to beach the ship, in order to get to the rudder, to make the repairs. With the help of a pilot from Guayaquil, we found an ideal spot. Across from the

Molicone there were two sandbars, with just the right space between them. The depth of water, when the tide was high, would allow us to maneuver the ship into position. John and I waded ashore, and placed two range markers to guide the positioning of the ship.

The two little tugboats, both on the starboard side, placed our ship in position, just up-river from the ranges. We drifted downstream with the current, and when the ranges came into alignment we started in. John let go the port anchor, while I gave the ship a shove with the main engine.

With the tugboats shoving as hard as they could, we touched bottom. John, on the bow, kept yelling to get the ship in farther. About the third yell, I gave a big shove with the main engine, and we thrust the Reefer about fifty feet onto the sandbar. With John yelling, "Stop, stop!" I stopped the main engine. I went forward with John, to see how the ship was situated. Everything looked great. We were in position.

As the sun went down, the tide ran out. Darkness descended over us, and the lights of Guayaquil came on. The ship settled into the sand, just as planned. When the river water was low, we lost the cooling water for the generators. The generators were shut down, and the ship was dead. There is a strange feeling to be on a ship with no sound, no light, and no power. The feeling is as if a town were to suddenly die. There are all of the streets and houses, but no life.

To deal with a new rudder, we had removed the five-ton chain falls from over the main generators. These were positioned in the stern to handle the weight of the rudder. The tackles from the lifeboats were also utilized in the rigging. We even took some of the cable from the mast. In the end, we were ready to handle a new rudder.

With lanterns and flashlights, we sat in the little skiffs and watched the rudder post emerge. Then the propeller materialized, and the water was still receding, we started work. Natives in dugout canoes cleared the water hyoscine with machetes. In the eerie glow of the lanterns, I watched the propeller shaft come out of the water. One tip of our three-bladed propeller was badly bent. Now our problem was compounded. By rigging the five-ton chain falls to the propeller, we pulled the propeller off. We then lowered it on the stern of the largest tugboat, where we had placed skids for this purpose. With a high tide, we retracted the Reefer, using the anchor and tugboats. This way we would not "hog" the ship.

After a few hours sleep, in the early morning we decided our next plan. At high water, we would skid the propeller off of the tugboat, and onto the sandy river bank. With the high tide in the afternoon, we put the plan into action. With skids, leverage and a lot of yelling Indians, we pulled and shoved the propeller up the river bank, above high water.

We made a bronze tip for the propeller. There was not enough heat from our two gas torches, so we had the Indians build a fire under the blade. This fire was fueled all night with hardwood. The following morning, John, Harold, and I gathered around and started welding again.

We finally had the propeller tip welded, and we knew the job was good. When we struck the propeller blades with a hammer, the pitch of the ring was the same. An insurance agent, from Lloyds of London, flew into Guayaquil. We took him across the river to the propeller, and he just hit the blades with a hammer, too.

We now put the propeller back on the ship. The rudder was ready, so we stepped the bottom of the rudder into the pentle bearing, and bolted the top flanges together. We retracted this time under our own power, with the rudder amidship.

By this time we had beached the Reefer seven times, and had consumed forty days. After a few days, our cargo was loaded, and once again we headed for the States. And this is how the rudder was lost, and how it was replaced on the M.V. Atlantic Reefer.

During the forty days we worked on the Reefer, the nights were spent ashore. John and I had a room in the Majestic Hotel, and were treated as royalty by Fred and Nada David. The thought never occurred to either John or me, to write a letter to our wives. So, for two months our wives didn't know where we were, or what we were doing.

A Trip Over the Andes

I sipped the warm milk, with the thick essence in it, and chewed on the hard, week-old biscuit they called breakfast. It was 0400 in the Majestic Hotel, one of the better ones in Guayaquil, Ecuador. I was due to leave on a bus — using the term loosely — bound for Quito. Fred David, the manager of the Majestic, had implored me not to take the bus.

"Take the airplane, like all the rest of the 'gringitos'" he'd urged. Fred told me horror stories of the bus sliding off the one-way dirt road. He explained about the wrecks high up in the mountains. Besides that, only Indians rode in the bus. His pleas were to no avail. I woke up the taxi driver, and for an extra sucre we were on our way to the bus station.

There was one dim 60-watt light bulb hanging over the door. When I tried to buy a bus ticket, I was told, "No hay, paga cuando usted entre." No tickets, pay when you enter. Well, I understood that. As I entered the bus with a lot of men, women and children, I looked for the goats and chickens, but there weren't any. These were all lowland Indians.

I took a seat next to a window, on the right side of the broken-down school bus. I think it was held together by prayer and bailing wire. The Indians filed slowly aboard with all of their bundles, but no one sat beside me. I was a novelty. They had a "gringito" on the bus with them.

Amid the yelling, hollering and the roar of the engine, we lurched onto the muddy road. We left Guayaquil bound for Daule, a small town twenty miles north of Guayaquil. Our route took us through the banana country, now and then a truck loaded with bananas would pass.

Arriving at Piedrahita, a town on the west side of the Daule River, everyone got out of the bus. At first I thought it was just a stop for a stretch, as I saw no bridge. Then with great dexterity the bus driver backed down a wet, dirt ramp onto an old American L.C.M., or Landing Craft Medium, which quartered into the cut in the river bank. With the bus in place, we all climbed back aboard.

The L.C.M. backed out into the river, and after safely getting across, headed into the same type of cut in the river bank on the other side. Again, all of the passengers disembarked and scampered up the river bank. As the spectators cheered, the bus emerged from the L.C.M. and sloshed up the dirt ramp. All of the passengers now pushed and shoved back into the bus. Once again we bounced along in the mud holes.

We arrived in Daule in a light rain, and had another river to cross, the Macui River, in much the same manner as the last crossing. The bus backed down the muddy ramp and onto a barge, then up the other side. The only difference was that this time the bus got stuck in the mud. Everyone disembarked, and I did, too.All of us pushed on the bus, trying to get it out of the mud. One of the Indians told me not to push on the bus, because this was not the work of white men, but I helped anyway. When the bus was free of the mud, we climbed back in and bounced on down the muddy road. This time there was an Indian in the seat beside me.

We now bumped along in a light rain toward the town of Babahoyo. In Babahoyo, some of the Indians got off, and yet others climbed in. There was a short pause here for strong coffee and homemade biscuits. As I drank my coffee, I studied the faces of the Indians. About 70 percent of the population of Ecuador are bush Indians. In this area they were lowland Indians, and most of them worked in the banana plantations. They are short and quite strong. A stem of bananas can weigh 125 pounds, and these Indians could carry two stems at a time. I have watched them jog for hours at a time, carrying 250 pounds on their shoulders.

From Babahoyo we bounced along the muddy road, stopping now and then to let someone on or off. As we passed little groups of people they would wave, and the driver would honk the horn. The natives are very friendly. At last we finally started pulling up the mountain.

By this time, the lowland Indians were almost off of the bus, and in their place were the highland Indians. These are the ones with large chests and the round, black hats. They had smiling, round faces, and were very friendly to me. There were two men behind me who asked if I would like to share some of their crackers. I told them yes, and took one. I picked the cracker up, and it was so delicate it shattered in my fingers. They all laughed and offered me another one. This time I was more careful, and was able to get it to my mouth. There was no salt, and no taste either, but then, I am not a connoisseur of fine foods. We climbed on up the mountain in low gears, and the time slowly went by.

The road up the mountain was a one-way dirt road, with wider places to pass now and then. The narrow road wound in and out of canyons, forever climbing. We were now enshrouded with clouds. I would look out the window and only see the bank alongside the road. The other side was only clouds.

Now and then, in the middle of nowhere, we would stop to let one of the passengers get off. Their houses were cut into the bank alongside the road. There would be a cut in the bank, then wood poles placed over the cut, and over that, soil. This abode would have a wood front, with one door but no windows. I have no idea how many people lived in one of these houses. I asked one of the Indians how high we were, he said about ten thousand feet.

We finally pulled out of the clouds and going over a mountain pass, dropped down into the town of Latacunga. Here our road intersected with the main Andean road, which runs north and south. Quito, the capital of Ecuador, was north of us, so that is the way we turned. Part of the road was gravel and some was asphalt, but the view was spectacular. Around us, and in the far distance, where high mountains. There were old volcano cones that rose to eighteen thousand feet. As the snow level is fifteen thousand feet, they look like huge chocolate ice-creme cones, topped off with white frosting.

Quito is about 45 miles north of Latacunga, and by now the sun had set. The light of a full moon came down through the thin, clear air and splashed over the valley. There was almost enough light to read by.

Ten miles north of Latacunga is the snow-capped cone of Cotopaxi. Our road took us north between Cotopaxi and the double cones of Iliniza. We bounced along the road, passing through the town of Machachi, nestled at the foot of Mt. Corazon. To the east, about twenty-five miles, we could see Mt. Antisana. Most of these mountains are snow-capped year-round.

The lights of Quito were before us, and it looked like our gallant conveyance would live long enough to arrive. Bidding adieu to my trusty cohorts, I hailed a taxi, which took me to the Savoy Hotel. The Savoy was recommended to me by an old, old man I knew in Guayaquil. Now I saw why. It was not only old, it was ancient. Pizarro must have slept here.

I entered this archaic structure and was met by the mayordomo, who bowed and granted my every wish. The dining room was closed, but coffee and a tuna sandwich were possible. As I'd had nothing to eat, except a few old biscuits, for the last sixteen hours, this meal was welcome and delicious.

Captain Radine, of the Atlantic Reefer, had flown up and retained a room for us. We sat in the room, and I detailed out the trip up the mountain. I told of crossing the rivers, and the houses cut in the bank of the road. By now, my get up and go, had got up and went. I stretched out on the wood plank covered with a quilt, which they call a bed, and was immediately fast asleep.

The morning broke bright and clear. After a fine breakfast, John and I hired a taxi for the day. With the taxi driver as our guide, we started another death defying ride over the back roads of Quito. Like all tourists, we ran up the side of a mountain, stopped, and looked at the spectacular view. This breathtaking view encompassed five gigantic snow cones — Cotacachi, 16,200 feet; Antisana, 18,700 feet; Cayambe, 19,000 feet; Cotopaxi 19,400, and Iliniza, rising to 17,300 feet. We realized we were standing in the foothills of Pachincha, which is 15,700 feet high.

The little hills around the base of these snow-capped mountains rose to 14,000 feet, but they are so small you don't notice them. The taxi driver pointed out ancient ruins and age-old trails until we told him to stop, we had to move on. Scrambling down the hill, we climbed in the old taxi, and once again were engulfed in a cloud of dust.

Driving north, we turned off the main road, and soon arrived at the Equatorial Monument. The name Ecuador comes from the word `equator'. As a navigator, I was interested in this history. The French surveyed the earth from about 1800 to 1837, utilizing all of the modern equipment of the period. At the termination of this project, they placed a monument here, marking the center of the earth.

John and I stepped out of the taxi and surveyed the monument. We were in a barren field that stretched to the hills. There were a few cows grazing, and a little broken-down curio shack, then nothing as far as the eye could see.

John and I stood on the monument, one foot in the north, and the other in the south. We jumped from the northern hemisphere to the southern hemisphere. We did all the things that tourists do, only there is one thing we knew that most tourists didn't know.

Although the French placed this monument here, there is another monument marking the center of the earth. This other monument was placed here thousands of years ago, so long ago the Indians have no mythology relating to how the marker arrived.

On Ecuadorian currency, two hills are printed. The ancient marker is located where these two hills meet. We could see the two hills in the distance, but it was too far to walk. There is no doubt the monument of the hills was placed there several thousand years ago. Could the great pathfinder, Maui, have been here? Was Aristothenes or Hecataeus of Alexandria involved in this survey, circa 400 B.C.? Well, no matter, John and I stood there and looked at time.

We drove north-east a few miles to Tabacundo to view the ruins. We were impressed, no doubt about that. The only trouble was, we didn't fully understand the sight. The taxi driver explained a lot of things to us, and we knew we were looking at an old civilization.

As our time was limited, with reluctance we headed back to Quito. We stopped a few minutes to inspect an ancient lime kiln, then on to the airport.

In the late afternoon, we boarded a large passenger plane, and with the four engines roaring, we lifted off of the runway. As the valley is 10,000 feet high, we had to circle to gain altitude. The second time around we headed west through a mountain pass. The pilot told us we were now at 13,000 feet, the only problem was, the ground was only about 500 feet below.

Arriving in Guayaquil just after sundown, we were in time for dinner with Fred and Nada. With an after-dinner drink, I told and retold the story of my trip over the Andes, in an old broken-down bus. I told of the mud, the crackers, and how friendly the natives were. Was the navigator Maui, who found the Hawaiian Islands in 231 B.C., here also? Who really put the ancient monument to the center of the earth in the Andean hills? Only the petroglyphs will tell.

Fat Rosa

I slowed the ship to dead slow, the pilot boat came alongside, and the Pilot laboriously climbed up the Jacob's ladder. We had just entered the harbor of Manzanillo, Mexico, and I was the Captain of the cargo ship, M.V. Maria Inez.

I turned the ship to dock port side to, and dropped the starboard anchor. By dropping the starboard anchor off of the dock, we could winch our bow out, and be underway without maneuvering the ship.

We were moored fore and aft to the dock, and the rat guards were in place. The gangplank was extended, and all of the officials and their helpers came aboard. The usual bottles of whiskey and cartons of cigarettes were handed out, and I gave my wristwatch to the Captain of the Port. The company bought the watches by the dozen, and I gave them out just as fast. At last, the officials left the ship, and we were calm again.

I'd first gone into Manzanillo in 1940, when I was a kid on an old ice boat, the Sea Boy. Those were the fishing boats where you pulled fish all day, then you packed each fish separately, by hand. By the time you had the fish packed, someone said, "Your watch, kid."

After World War II, I was in and out of this sea port four or five times a year. Now I was the Captain on a refrigerated cargo ship, hauling bananas and limes from the states of Jalisco, Michoacan and Colima. Needless to say, as Captain of the ship, I had prestige and some clout.

Several of the local businessmen had small children. The children were sick, and they couldn't eat the rough food. I smuggled in Gerber's baby food by the case. Canned food was a big item, but the baby food really made friends with the people. I was well known by businessmen, port officials and longshoremen.

The loading dock, for us, was by the town square. On Saturday nights, the men would walk around in one direction, while the women would walk in the other direction. In the center

87

of the square there was a raised bandstand, below this was a soft drink stand run by a lady named Martha. I would sit on the bridge of the ship and watch the people promenade around the square.

If I tired of this, I would go to an ice cream parlor just across the street, and enjoy a cold, refreshing ice cream. I was also known to step into a cantina now and then.

It so happened that when I was here in 1940, on the old ice boat Sea Boy, all of the fishermen went to the same cantina, One-Eyed Joe's. I had met One-Eyed Joe at that time. Joe had a nice cantina in the city limits, but as years went by, for obvious reasons, his business was put out of town.

In these cantinas there is a large scattering of fallen doves. These impecunious sirens of the shore smiled sweetly, and picked up your change for a drink. They could pluck quicksilver from a thick carpet with their fingers. But some did have a heart of gold. Fat Rosa was one of these. She weighed in at about two hundred pounds, and was two axe handles across the stern. You would have to reach twice to get around her once. If nothing else, Rosa was honest. She would ask before she picked up your money. With a ready smile and a quick hand, she would greet you in English.

Now it so happened that our Chief Engineer, Charlie, could top the scales about sixty pounds over Fat Rosa. Charlie's wife had died many years before, and Charlie was a loner. He had accumulated very little in his long life at sea. Most of his hard-earned loot had surreptitiously vanished in seaport towns across the earth.

When Charlie walked into One-Eyed Joe's cantina, Fat Rosa shook like Jell-O, and it was love at first sight. She turned on her charm, blinked her eyes, and Charlie was overcome with amour. As she walked away, she looked like a gunny sack full of snakes. You knew something was wiggling, but you didn't know what. This harpy of the beach had tossed the net over our chief engineer. Rosa didn't have to pick up the change from the bar. Charlie gave it to her. In fact, the Chief was so infatuated with Rosa that he gave her a good deal of money. Charlie even bought a king-sized bed for her. It was the only king-size bed in One-Eye's cantina. I always knew where to find Charlie when we were in Manzanillo.

I was on deck talking to the loading foreman, about the cargo, when Charlie walked up.

"Hey Ed, what's this kid trying to tell me?" asked Charlie. Looking behind him I saw a small urchin, a real chamaco. I asked him what he wanted, and he told me this sad story.

This small boy was Rosa's little brother. Rosa had sent him to tell Charlie that she was in jail, and he had to get her out. When I told Charlie that his light-o'-love was in the pokie, the carcel, he jumped into action.

He turned to me and said, "We have to get her out!"

How did I get involved in this?

Charlie and I marched off the ship with the emancipation of the female world thrust upon our shoulders. We marched into the office that housed the dignitaries of the town, and I became a golden-tongued orator. I excelled in Spanish oration that day. Then we all sat down, three of them and two of us.

It seems that Charlie's rosie-cheeked girlfriend had been picked up because she hadn't paid for her license to ply her illicit trade. It was ten dollars per annum to ply the oldest trade on earth. Fat Rosa hadn't paid her ten dollars, so she was in the pokie. Not only was she in, but so were about another twenty of these beauties.

I explained all of this to Charlie, and we decided the only gentlemanly thing to do would be to bail out all of these creatures of the night. I turned to the three officials and started a long harangue about the ladies taking up the room in the jail, when there were a lot of very bad bandidos that should be there, instead. Not only that, but look at the food the government had to feed them. Last, but not least, look at the happiness they were suppressing.

The officials agreed with me, and we all wisely nodded our heads. But what about the assessment for the girls? At long last I came up with three twenty-dollar bills, three bottles of Scotch whisky and three cartons of cigarettes. We all smiled and they said this was a very wise decision. But could I hurry? It was siesta time.

Charlie and I scrambled out of the office, and headed to the ship. We picked up the payola from the ship and went back to the office. With a twenty-dollar bill, a bottle of Scotch and a carton of cigarettes for each, the order was given to release the ladies of jaded character. We shook hands all around. I gave each one a new wrist watch for good luck, then Charlie and I went out of the building. We felt that we would be immortalized, enshrined in the hearts of these frail sisters.

As it turned out, we were almost immortalized in the town!

When Charlie and I stepped out of the building, we stood in shock. Surrounded by about twenty ladies of the night, we couldn't get back into the building. They thanked us, and thanked us some more, then informed us they didn't have transportation out to Joe's. As the businessmen looked on, Charlie and I managed to round up about four taxicabs, and like a great herd of cattle, the roundup was on. We stuffed these Jezebels into the taxis, and had to pay the taxi, too. Then, down the road they lurched.

Charlie and I sauntered down the block, smiling and nodding to the businessmen. I could have made mixed drinks for ten years with the icy stares we received from the women. We went into the first cantina we came to, we were going to calm our nerves. The bartender bought us the first round, then one by one the businessmen in the area entered, and bought a round.

We did get back to the ship in good shape, but believe me, I will always remember Fat Rosa.

Mexican Gold

I stirred the ice floating in my drink and looked at Jerry. We were sitting in the Court Room Bar in La Jolla, California, and he had just told me a fantastic story. Jerry's father, "Honest" Jim Franks, had just returned from a trip into Baja, California. Honest Jim had looked at some bars of solid gold, and was now in San Francisco with the Minister of Finance of China.

Jerry Franks had been a hot fighter pilot in World War II, flying front line support for General Patton. Most of Jerry's flying had been at tree-top level, knocking out German tanks, railroad trains, oil tanks, and anything else in his way. Jerry was an extremely fine pilot with an unlimited, multi-engine license.

Honest Jim had been financed by some people in Tucson, Arizona to go down into Baja and look at gold bars. After he saw the gold, he came back to San Diego and told his son, Jerry. Then Honest Jim went to San Francisco to meet with the government official from China. Jim's idea was to sell this gold to China for sixty dollars an ounce. Now, Jim wanted his son, Jerry, to take one or two men with him, fly down to Baja and load the gold into an airplane, and fly it out.

I was currently the Captain of a little cargo ship called the Maria Inez, which made the run from San Diego to Manzanillo, Mexico, bringing back limes and bananas. In 1953 we didn't have the books and maps of Baja that are available today. Most of the country was unknown to the general public. Jerry, prematurely gray, his face crossed with deep lines from the strain of W.W. II, waved to the waitress for another round.

"This is what I think," he said as he paid for the drinks. "We'll take Bob MacKouski with us, and each of us take two suitcases. We'll fly down to where Dad says the gold is, and put the gold into the suitcases. Then we'll fly to La Paz, pay off the officials and fly up to Tucson. When we hit Tucson, we'll be home free."

I took a sip from my drink, shook my head and said, "What a

stupid idea. First off, we can only carry a very small amount of the gold. Second, when we land in Tucson and the Customs open the suitcases, we'll all land in jail."

Jerry leaned forward and almost whispered, "No, no, the Tucson people have the Customs all paid off. No problem. We'll make six or eight trips."

"Jerry," I said, twirling the ice in my drink again, "you have this all wrong. I've been in the business for a long time, you know that, and what you just said is rank amateurishly."

Jerry leaned back, looked across the table and said, "Well, how would you get a ton of gold out of Mexico?"

I finished the drink, waved at the waitress for another and said, "First, I'd have the Tucson people contact my principals, and use the Maria Inez. I'd take the Maria Inez to say, San Quintin. Not up in the bay, but east of the cape. There's a dirt road that runs along the beach, just north of El Pabellon. I'd truck the gold down to the beach and load it on the ship."

Jerry leaned forward and in a whisper asked, "Then what would you do?"

"The way you do it is simple enough. Move the gold aboard the Maria Inez. Then cut out some of the planking from the ship's skin. From the outside to the inside, the hull is about twenty-eight inches. This means the ribs must be about twenty inches deep." I took a sip of Scotch and Jerry nodded agreement. "Then I'd stash the gold alongside the ribs and replank the skin."

Once again Jerry nodded agreement. "But where would you go then, and how would you make the new planking look old?"

In answer I said, "First off, I would have cleared the ship for Panama, to take on bunkers. On second thought, we could go to Talara, Peru. Standard Oil has a station there, and number two oil."

I leaned back and gave this idea a little thought. "I've been in there for fuel before, nothing strange about that. Then you run about a hundred and thirty miles up to Puerto Bolivar, Ecuador and load fruit."

I looked at the mural behind the bar of the twelve judges presiding over this bar. I thought it odd that the face of one was a general contractor and the face of another was a roofing contractor, both here in La Jolla.

I looked back at Jerry and said, "I think it would be better to go to Talara. There's a little pier there, we would tie up starboard side to. We could call our principals and get an order to change our destination to, say, the Marquesas."

"How far is that?"

I thought a bit. "As I remember, it's about three thousand miles, just about due west of Talara. We'd have enough fuel."

I let this idea run around in Jerry's head for a while. "Not only that," I added, "but if you rub the skin of a banana on fresh paint, it will age it in minutes; the latex does it."

"Well, okay. If it worked like this, then where would you go and how would you get to China?"

I looked at Jerry and said, "Now listen carefully. We clear for Talara, get a change of sailing orders and proceed to the Marquesas for fuel. Then get another change of orders and proceed to Wake Island for fuel. We keep getting change orders from our principals, and wind up in Shanghai, China."

Jerry smiled and added, "You've got a plan, no doubt about that."

"And, I'll tell you the last thing. When we get to China with the gold we're all shot dead and they take the gold. Count me out." With that, I picked up my drink and leaned back.

A full minute went by without a word, only the general noise of the establishment. I could see that Jerry was thinking, trying to punch holes in the plan.

I looked across the table and said, "Jerry, let me tell you something about gold. Here in the U.S. it's thirty-five dollars an ounce. They're taking gold out of Ecuador by the kilo, and shipping it to Europe for forty dollars an ounce. The Indians steal it."

"And here's some more," I added. "There's an old rusty freighter that anchors in Lake Gatun, Panama. He anchors for repairs maybe for six months, then he heads for Venezuela. He breaks down just off Barranquilla, Columbia and a tugboat tows him back to Panama."

"How can he make any money breaking down all the time?" Jerry asked.

"It's the gold." I answered. "When I worked in the Caribbean around Santa Marta and Barranquilla, there was no place to go but the bars and joints. One night I was drinking with a sailor from that freighter. He had a round piece of gold, like our silver dollars. It only had a number stamped on it. This is how the gold goes from Ecuador to Europe. It's loaded on the freighter in Lake Gatun, then to Barranquilla. From there to Europe."

With that long-winded tirade, I took another drink of Scotch and watched Jerry's face. I looked at the faces on the mural behind the bar, and wondered just how long one had to drink here to become one of the judges.

"The Indians bring the gold out in a quill . . . you know, a big, long feather. They cut the end off of the feather, fill it with gold, put a cap on it and sell the quill for about a dollar."

"You have a working plan, no doubt about that. I'll tell my Dad about it. He'll be back in a week or two," Jerry said as he stood up. I dropped a generous tip for the waitress, and followed him to the door.

"Don't forget to tell your Dad that I want no part of it," I said, as we headed for our cars.

That night I dreamed of taking the Maria Inez into some bay in Baja, of loading gold bullion into a lower hold, heading south and stashing the gold in the ship's hull. I woke up when we got to China. That was a bad dream!

I made another six or eight trips to Manzinillo for bananas and limes, then one day my boss told me we were out of business. The San Diego Banana Company was broke. He told me to take the Maria Inez and put it alongside the Atlantic Reefer in Martinolich Shipyard.

We took the crew off of the Maria Inez and put them on the

Atlantic Reefer, then we all headed south. We discharged the Mexicans in Manzinillo and departed for Talara, Peru. We discharged several good men there, and after we took on bunkers we ran up to Guayaquil, Ecuador. With a full load of fruit, we sailed for Miami, Florida, by way of Panama.

Maybe six months went by, and we were hauling fruit into Galveston, Texas. When we took departure one day, the Coast Guard came onboard the ship for a full search. They searched the ship and when we proceeded out the channel, a Coast Guard cutter followed us out to the sea buoy.

We hauled in fruit for another three or four trips, then one day an Immigration officer in Galveston told us what it was all about.

The Immigration Officer explained to Capt. Radine and me, there was a man named Lewellen they were trying to catch. He was on the F.B.I.'s list of the ten most wanted men. Because this man had been around Las Vegas, Nevada and my boss had some interest there, the F.B.I. thought he might be trying to get out of the country on the Atlantic Reefer.

None of us knew Mr. Lewellen by sight, name or fame. We told the Immigration man to get him on the Reefer, and we would take him out to sea. That way, there wouldn't be any charge for lawyers or court costs. The Immigration guy didn't see the situation our way.

At last, by word around the docks, we learned that Lewellen had bought the Maria Inez, which was now in a shipyard somewhere in Oregon or Washington being outfitted.

The next time I heard of the Maria Inez, she was seaworthy and on her way to Panama. By some strange quirk of fate, she had engine trouble and had to go into a harbor in Baja California. She anchored in the harbor all night, and by daylight was out to sea again. I thought of the Mexican gold, of Honest Jim Franks and the Tucson gambling organization. This sounded like the plan I had laid out for Jerry that night in the Court Room bar.

We lost track of the Maria Inez after she cleared Baja. As the weeks went by, we heard a strange story unfold. Our information came from the docks in Panama, from the longshoremen in Ecuador, and even a story by a man in Talara, Peru, who worked for Standard Oil.

This man, who worked for Standard Oil in Talara, said he remembered a ship called the Maria Inez taking on bunkers some months back. He said one of the crew told him they were going to Tahiti, or somewhere in the western Pacific. The man with Standard Oil said the Maria Inez had a change of destination to pick up a cargo. He said he would like to have sailed with them, but he was stuck with Standard Oil of Peru.

We didn't hear any more about the Maria Inez for several months, then one day we took a load of fruit to Long Beach, California. Capt. Radine lived in San Pedro, so he went home. My home was in San Diego, so I went to the closest bar. I met a man there who had a wild story about a small freighter, called the Maria Inez. I bought a round of drinks and listened to this strange and fantastic tale.

This guy had worked for Van Camp Sea Food Company in American Samoa. Van Camp had fishing boats around the area, fishing yellowfin tuna. There was a story around Samoa about a little freighter that was out in the Gilbert Islands, or the Solomons, and a fire broke out in the engine room. The crew couldn't save the ship, so they took to the lifeboats. The ship burned and sank off of some islands. The crew rowed to the closest island and went ashore.

Now in World War II, the United States Navy bypassed a lot of the little islands, kind of a leapfrog idea. This island happened to be one of the islands that was passed over. There had been some Japanese army personal stationed there, but they were gone.

The natives on this island were cannibalistic, like many of the out-of-the-way islands. There were some missionaries on the island, trying to save the souls of these fat cannibals, but to no avail. One by one the crew of this little freighter were killed and eaten by the natives, with the exception of one — the Captain.

The Captain's eyes were very poor, and he wore glasses like

the bottoms of Coca-Cola bottles. He could have used them like a magnifying glass to make fire. For some reason the natives didn't eat him, but gave him to the missionaries. In turn, the missionaries admonished the natives for cannibalism, but sent the Captain back to Samoa. From there, he was sent to Los Angeles, California, and is now in the asylum for the insane at Norwalk, a raving maniac!

The first part of this story I know as a fact, but the latter part is the raving of a barroom drunk. Or is it? Besides the Maria Inez, there are three other ships I know of with the same engine room. There is the Atlantic Reefer, Anaugua and Pacific Reefer, until she sank.

The Pacific Reefer sank just off of Cedros Island, Baja California. She was diesel-electric, with two main generators. Fire broke out on the exhaust manifold of the starboard engine. The ship's fire and bilge pumps were centered in the forward part of the lower engine room, right where the fire broke out. There was no way to get to the pumps, no fire fighting equipment, so she burned.

Because the Pacific Reefer was sunk by fire in the engine room, the Maria Inez could have sunk the same way. The fire started around the exhaust manifold which, on the starboard engine, is on the inboard side. That put the fire right over the ship's fire and bilge plumps. I know that's how it was on the Pacific Reefer, because Captain John Radine was on board at that time.

Well, that's my story of the Maria Inez. That story is a little close to me, because I was Captain of her for a period of time. I wonder if Lewellen got Honest Jim's gold out of Baja? Or, is all that gold laying on the bottom of the ocean off of some island in the Solomons? Those islands were named after King Solomon, because at that time people thought that's where the gold of King Solomon was hidden. Maybe the only gold there is Mexican Gold.

The Slow Rising Yeast.

The small cargo ship, Maria Inez, was tied up at Martinolich Ship Yard in San Diego, California. I was the Captain on this little bucket, and we had been tied up for general repairs almost a month. I was talking to John Radine, the Captain of the Atlantic Reefer, when Anton Martinolich, who owned both ships, walked up the gangplank.

Mr. Martinolich, or Tony as everyone called him, poured a cup of old coffee and sat down. John and I sat down at the galley table with him.

"I'll tell you what I have in mind," he said. "I'm going to start another company, the San Diego Banana Company." He took a sip of his coffee and made a face. "Why don't you guys ever make a new pot of coffee?" With a dour expression, Tony set the cup down and continued. "Both of you are ready for sea, and I have Captain Seamack bringing the Anaugua around from the Caribbean. I've started a business in Manzinillo, Mexico, to haul bananas and limes out of the states of Jalisco, Michoacan and Colima."

Tony stood up and started to pace the deck. We could see that his mind was going a mile a minute. He stopped, turned around and said, "John, your crew is all set, but Ed needs a crew on the Maria Inez. Ed, you and John take a skeleton crew with you, go down to Manzinillo and pick up a crew." That sounded good to us. It was time to get back out to sea and make some money.

Tony had said all he wanted to say, and he marched off of the ship. John turned to me and said, "That's it, lets move." I grabbed a pencil and paper for notes, while John made a new pot of coffee. We both sat down to think this out.

As Manzinillo is only about a four day run, we would only need three men in the engine room. We had an automatic pilot, so three men on deck would handle the watches. A cook was a necessity. In the shipyard were some men that knew this engine room. John and I went ashore and into the machine shop. We talked to

Bill Loverich, Stacy and Moon, the electrician. They said they would like to take a couple of weeks off with pay.

It so happened that Bob Martinolich, Tony's brother, was walking through the yard. John spotted him and called him over. He didn't do any work anyhow. John asked him if he would sail as cook. He said he would love to, and he could cook, too. Neither John nor I had ever known of Bob cooking, but at least he could do the dishes and clean up.

I asked a friend of mine, Bob MacKouski, if he would like to go for a vacation, and he said he would love it. That gave us a skeleton crew, three engine room, three deck and a cook. That was enough to run the ship for a few days. We all helped each other anyhow.

I looked in my file for the galley, and found an old food order. I gave the list to a store on India Street, and they delivered it. I cleared the ship and we were ready to depart for Manzinillo, Mexico.

Elmer Don, a yard foreman for Tony, came walking out on the pier, and came aboard for coffee. "I hear you're going to Mexico and looking for some help," he said. I told him that we could use all the help we could get, so come along. Elmer brought his gear aboard.

We cleared San Diego harbor about sundown, and I set a course inside the Coronado Islands. When we were clear of the Coronados, I changed the course for outside of Cedros Island, and went to bed.

Daylight broke bright and clear, with an easy following swell. We were about forty miles off San Quintin Bay, and about eight hours run north of Cedros Island. I went below to see how Bob was doing in the galley.

Everything looked great. Bob had bacon and eggs with toast. I picked up a plate and sat down to breakfast. One by one the men straggled in and sat down. We all had bacon and eggs. That's all there was.

We merrily rolled south, and at noon we had soup and a sandwich for lunch. Dinner came along and we had bacon and eggs, again. No one complained, we just ate dinner and went about our work. At Cedros Island I changed course, and went back to bed.

Once again daylight broke warm and clear. We were off the south end of Ballenas Bay and well clear. I went below for breakfast and looked in on Bob. Bob was cooking bacon and eggs again. I made a remark to Bob about having the same food and that we should change it. In the end, I consumed bacon and eggs with toast and coffee. When the other men came in, there was a little grumbling, but they ate breakfast anyhow.

We sailed by Magdalana Bay and again we had soup and sandwiches for lunch. Several of the men asked me about the food. It was all the same. Food is the only good thing you have at sea. All else is just monotonous work. A cook at sea has to vary the menu. If you have bacon and eggs one day, then you have pancakes and fruit the next. There has to be change, or the crew becomes grouchy. I decided to have a talk with Bob.

Bob and I leaned on the lower deck railing, just outside of the galley, and I explained to him our little problem. I told him there would be no bacon and eggs for dinner, nor would there be bacon and eggs for breakfast. I told him I would help him anyway I could, but we had to make a change. This was imperative.

We found some steaks in the freezer, so we had steak and potatoes for dinner. We opened up some canned vegetables, and with a little fruit, this rounded out our dinner. That night we went to bed happily, and as we sailed by Cape San Lucas, I made another course change.

The Gulf of California is about two hundred and seventy miles wide at the mouth, and we had breakfast in the middle of it. Daylight broke and I checked our position with my sextant, took a look around and went below. Bob was in the galley, rattling pots and pans.

I said good morning and stepped into the galley. "Well Bob, what's for breakfast today," I asked.

"How about pancakes and some sausage, with fruit," he

replied.

"Let's get started!"

We looked in the cupboard for the pancake mix, and couldn't find any. We looked in the food locker, on the shelves and back again in the cupboards. I couldn't believe there was not one box of pancake mix. I guess a real cook makes everything from scratch. Well, I decided Bob and I would do the same.

Bob brought out a large mixing bowl and spoon. I brought out some flour, milk, and eggs. Bob had some bacon frying for the oil, and I was looking for the salt, sugar and baking powder. I know that a little salt and sugar would change the taste. That's why they're called pancakes. For real light, fluffy, and beautiful cakes, you have to add about a teaspoon of baking powder.

Bob and I looked high and low, but there was not a can of baking powder, and that was final. We did find some blocks of slow-rising yeast and decided that a real cook would use yeast. I scrapped off some of the slow-rising yeast into a cup with milk, stirring it around to make a paste, so we could fold it into the pancake mix. I finally had a cup full of milky paste.

In all sincerity, Bob and I mixed the material up and let it set for about fifteen minutes. The mix did seem to raise a little, but not much. Bob poured some of the mix onto the grill and we watched. The cake didn't rise like we thought it should. It looked about like a tortilla, but still in our imagination we were hoping it would.

It was full daylight when John Radine walked into the galley and said, "Well, what do we have today?"

"Pancakes with lots of crisp bacon, topped off with some chilled fruit," I answered.

"Well, I don't want any of that. Just give me some bacon and eggs, scrambled." With that retort, John walked over to the table in the mess room and sat down. I tried my best, but some people are set in their ways. Bob scrambled up three eggs, put on some bacon and took it into John.

I thought about those pancakes, so I asked Bob to give me

some scrambled eggs on top of one pancake. When Bob dished it up for me, I ate it in the galley and not the mess room. I didn't want anyone to see me.

The next in was Elmer Don, tall, black hair and easy going. He was standing a deck watch. With a big smile he asked, "What's for breakfast?"

I told him pancakes and bacon with chilled fruit. Elmer said, "That sounds great!" He ate three pancakes and came back for three more. Elmer toped the six cakes off with a lot of bacon and chilled fruit, then went up to the main deck.

After Elmer, the rest of the crew traipsed in one by one. They all ate pancakes with a lot of bacon and fruit. I finished my eggs and one pancake then returned to the bridge. Bobby Mac came up on the bridge and we sat there talking. The rest of the men just relaxed till there watch.

I stretched out in my bunk, behind the pilot house and started reading in a book. The morning passed, and I went down for a little bite of lunch. With only eight men on board, it was extremely quiet. With Bob in the galley, one man on the bridge and one man in the engine room, it seemed like a ghost ship of some type. We just sailed along, with no one in sight.

I talked a little with Bob, then John came in for a sandwich. No one else came in for lunch. The watch changed at noon, and I went up on the bridge to see how we were doing. Elmer Don walked up to me and said, "Ed, I have stomach cramps really bad. You can't believe the gas on my stomach. Could I skip my watch?"

I told him to go lie down, and not to worry about standing watch. It wasn't an hour later that Stacy came up, and told me about stomach cramps. Then Bobby Mac walked in, and it was the same story. Moon came up to the bridge and had the same problem.

In the space of two hours all of the crew had stomach cramps and a tremendous amount of stomach gas. Everyone except John Radine, Bob Martinolich and I had stomach cramps. That slow-rising yeast in the pancakes had started to rise, but in their stomachs. These men were all lying in their bunks, groaning and moaning.

John Radine went below and stood the engine room watch and I took the deck, watch while Bob, our cook, finished up the dishes. I could see what had happened, and when Bob came up to the bridge we had a little talk. We agreed not to tell a soul that we had put slow rising yeast in the pancakes.

We entered the harbor at Manzinillo, Mexico, the next day. As we moored alongside the dock, the crew slowly came out on deck and looked around. We picked up a crew of good seaman and engineers, then loaded a cargo of bananas and limes. In a few days we were north bound. To this day, the story of the slow-rising yeast has never been told.

In the years to come, John and I crossed the Caribbean over one hundred times. Bobby Mac made a fifty-three-day trip to Ecuador with us, for a load of fruit. The rest of the men went back to work in the shipyard. Only Bob Martinolich and I know who put the slow rising yeast in the pancakes.

15 tons of heavy 2 Pole – Chicken of the Sea.
Harold Morgan Captain. Galapagos Islands.

Larry Labruzzi, John Princeiapto, Frank Valin with heavy
3 Pole.

Light 3 Pole. Chicken of the Sea. Jack Vore lead man.

50 tons of Skipjack Tuna. Corsair, Melvin Morgan Capt.

1200 lbs. Northern Bluefin Tuna. Purse Seiner "Elizebath C. J."
off of the Azores.

M. V. Corsair, converted "Y. P." Melvin Morgan Capt.

Making gear on Chicken of the Sea. Bud Morgan with hat, "Tucker" right foreground. Poles in canopy.

Atlantic Reefer. John Radine Capt. Salmon boats on deck.
Going to Alaska.

Atlantic Reefer. Loading doors on starboard side. Speedboat
under canvas. Going to Ecuador.

Capt. John Radine and Ed Suman. Atlantic Reefer.

Harold Kenyon, Charlie Gannet, John Radine, Ed Suman.

Maria Inez when Tony bought her. Ed Suman Capt.

Maria Inez loading fruit in Manzinillo, Mexico.

Ed Suman with some extremely bad fruit.

El Cotopaxi, Ecuador. Snow line is 15000 feet.

Equatorial monument north of Quito, Ecuador.

Rare picture of Fred and Nada David in mountain chalet. Ecuador.

Atlantic Reefer and other ship in Panama Canal.

BOOK III

Smuggling

The Great Handkerchief Drop

Passing between Santa Clara Island and Puna Island, I set a course northerly for Mandragon Island, where we stopped. We were just off the Puna Pilot Station at the mouth of the Guayas River, Ecuador. The idea was to place the ship as far from the Puna Pilot Station as possible, and still have the pilot come out. The longer it took for the shore boat to bring out the pilot, and armed guards, the better. I was first officer on the M. V. Atlantic Reefer, a refrigerated cargo ship, whose primary function was hauling bananas from South America to the United States.

About every three weeks we made a round trip from Galveston, Texas, through the Panama canal, then to some port in Ecuador. With a load of about 20,000 stems of bananas, we would then retrace our route back to the United States. We had been on this "banana run" for several years. Like all other ships, we had a little "business" on the side. You might say we were smugglers.

Smuggling is the system of avoiding the payment of taxes to the government. Some 80% of all cargos that land in South America are smuggled. The great bulk of smuggling is with the white-collar politicians. A ship docks, the cargo is off-loaded, and with a kickback to the big politician, the cargo manifest is signed. Nothing is paid to the government, no taxes are paid. If you work or live in these countries, then you understand the system. We had worked here long enough to understand.

I was down on the main deck, starboard side, where some 75 cases of cigarettes were stacked, ready to go over the side. The dugout canoes came out of the jungle, with two Indians in each. The canoes paddled up to the starboard side, and one of the men climbed aboard. This man, with a big handful of money, purchased as many cases of cigarettes as would fit in his canoe. This business was strictly cash, no credit. We bought the cigarettes for $50. 00 a case, and they went over the side at $95. 00 a case.

While this "business" was going on below, Capt. John was on the port side of the bridge, watching the shore boat approach. John watched the shore boat on the port side, and I watched the "business" on the starboard side. When the shore boat, with the boarding party, was close, Capt. John yelled down to me to "clear the decks." With this signal, "business" stopped. Any cases left on deck were once again locked in the ship's storeroom. Stepping to the typewriter, I typed the exact number of cases in the storeroom, on the ship's store list.

As the shore boat came along the port side, the Indians in their canoes faded into the jungle on the starboard side. When the armed guards rushed over to the starboard side, only jungle was to be seen. The ship shuddered as the main engines turned over, and we were underway. The guards came up to the bridge and blustered around, while the stoic pilot watched the river. John and I soothed the rumpled feelings of the guards. In a few minutes all was forgotten, and the Atlantic Reefer was headed up the Guayas River.

From the Puna Pilot Station to Guayaquil is about thirty miles, up the Guayas River. The town was started by pirates where the Guayas divides. As tidal action has a big effect on this river, the square-rigged ships of the British Navy, or any other navy, had to wait for the flood tide to sail up the river. The delay would give the pirates time to hide in the jungle, so the British never did catch the pirates. To these descendants of pirates, stealing is a way of life.

The Guayas River, fed by the Daule and the Bodegas Rivers, winds its way down to Puna Island. This river is not straight, like the chart shows. We made our way up the river, and talked to the pilot and guards, just small talk. Then about five miles south of Guayaquil, the river makes a hard turn to the left, then a hard turn to the right. Now we were on the final reach to Guayaquil.

When a ship enters this turn, it is out of sight, with only the jungle on either side. As we started into this turn, the Captain asked the pilot and guards to follow him below. There, in the ship's office, he would give each one a bottle of whiskey and a carton of cigarettes.

We approached the first turn, and there were two dugout canoes on the right-hand side. These canoes had two men in each, and were about 50 yards apart. Standing on the starboard wing of the bridge, I looked aft at a crewman, leaning against the rail. This man had a string in his hand. The crewman acted as if he were half asleep, but in reality, he was watching me. The string ran down and into the loading port below.

One of our crewmen would be on the wheel, steering the ship up the river. He knew the river as well as the pilot, so I didn't have a problem there. When we swung into the turn, I gave the signal to the man in the stern. He gave a pull on the string that led to the loading port below. The port opened, and a large waterproof bag came out of the port, splashing into the river. Then another waterproof bag follow.

As the loading port closed, the two canoes converged on the floating bags and rolled them aboard. The two Indians turned around in the canoe and paddle back into the jungle, lost to view. This operation only took about two minutes. Then a swing to starboard, and we were on the final approach to the anchorage at Guayaquil.

These waterproof bags contained several hundred dozens of handkerchiefs. This is how we took handkerchiefs into Ecuador. Undoubtedly there were other systems, utilized by other ships, but this was our system.

In months to come, the guards were told not to leave the bridge, and watched our every move. Our system did not change. The Captain would go below and the guards would stay on the bridge and watch. The Captain would return to the bridge with several bottles of whiskey, and cartons of cigarettes for the guards. He then called the guards to the port side, where they received their booze. While the guards were on the port side, I would give the signal on the starboard. The handkerchiefs went over the side, anyway.

The guards complained and demand that we stop the ship. I explained that we could not stop in the river, it is too dangerous.

Not only that, but the bags only contained garbage. The guards could only watch the canoes fade into the jungle.

The next day, as we were taking on cargo in Guayaquil, a kindly old man came aboard. This little old man had a big bag of money, for he had the handkerchief business of Guayaquil. We sat in the ship's office and counted out the money. After a drink of good Scotch whiskey, and lots of handshaking and hugs, he departed for town.

With a full load of bananas, we started down the river. The pilot and guards received their pay off, and everyone was happy. Now and then we would pass a dugout canoe. The man in it give us a friendly wave, for he was a "businessman," too. And this is how Guayaquil, Ecuador received handkerchiefs for the wealthy.

A Bad Trip to Esmeraldas, Ecuador

We were dockside in Panama, taking on bunkers and water, when a well-dressed, dark-complected man came aboard. He and the Captain went into the ship's office, and when they came out, the Captain told me we would take a cargo of cigarettes and whiskey to Guayaquil, Ecuador. This entrepreneur was a smuggler!

In short order, two large moving vans drove up on the dock, and out came the gravity conveyers. We loaded more than 100 cases of cigarettes and 150 cases of whiskey. This merchandise is purchased from the "free zone" in Panama. This is a zone, or area, where cargos are stored for transshipment. There is no taxation on commodities in this free zone.

The sun was getting low in the west when the pilot came on board, and we let go fore and aft. With a prolonged blast on the ship's whistle, we cleared the dock. We proceeded out the channel, and the pilot boat came along the port side. One of the crew came up to the bridge, with a letter from the ship's broker in Panama.

The Captain opened the sealed letter and read the contents. Turning to me he said, "We have a slight problem. Instead of Guayaquil, we are going to Esmeraldas. " The Captain asked the pilot to take us to the anchorage, so we could stall for time. We needed time to think this problem out. We had a cargo of contraband, and now our destination had been changed! The contraband needed to be off-loaded here in Panama.

Dropping anchor in Panama Bay, we explained our problem to the pilot. All pilots have been Captains of their own ships for a minimum of ten years, and understand problems of shipping. He said he would be glad to take a letter to the supplier of the cargo. I typed out a letter, explaining why we could not take the cargo to Guayaquil, and the pilot took it ashore.

Several hours went by, and there was no answer to our letter.

We watched for a signal from shore, but saw nothing. The Captain gave the order to pull the anchor and get underway. Once again we were headed south, bound for Ecuador.

Esmeraldas, Ecuador is about 450 miles south of Panama, and another 200 miles to Point Santa Elena, where we had contacts to off-load the contraband. It was impossible to run 200 miles south, unload the cargo, and run 200 north, and still keep our time schedule to load cargo at Esmeraldas. In a situation like this, you have every right to throw the cargo overboard to save the ship. The well-dressed, dark-complected man from Ecuador was on board to protect his cargo, so we all sat down and had a little talk.

This "businessman" had his life savings in this cargo, and he was heartbroken. We decided we would hide the contraband somewhere on the ship, and when we came out of Esmeraldas, try to off-load to some contraband runner. With this plan in mind, I looked over the ship. Where to hide 100 cases of cigarettes and 150 cases of whiskey? Then I found the right place.

On the second deck down, in the bow, were the chain lockers. This is an area where you flake-out the anchor chain, so it is ready to run out again, a storage area. As we would use the port anchor, I could hide the cargo in the starboard locker, and also in the area dividing the two chain lockers. There was also a paint locker that would take 50 cases. The Captain listened to the plan, and said it was all right with him.

As we rolled along southbound in a calm sea, one by one we lifted the cases out of the forward cargo hold and carried them forward. One by one, we lowered them down into the chain locker and placed them as tight as we could. Keeping the port locker clear so the chain could run out, and leaving a small passageway, we sealed off the locker. Then for good luck, we covered the access hatch, too. Now all we had to do was keep a straight face, and no one talk.

The mouth of the Esmeraldas River is an old volcano, so to make landfall you lower the anchor, and when you fetch-up on the far side, you are anchored. With flags flying we anchored in the mouth of the river and waited for the boarding party. The boat from shore was on its way out, with all the dignitaries, and once more I cautioned the crew about talking, or taking bribes!

The shore boat was alongside, and the boarding party with their helpers came aboard. We all sat down at a large table, and as the paper work went around, I brought out a bottle of whiskey and a carton of cigarettes for each person. We had been in this port many times and were well liked. Then came the problem.

The new problem was this. Along with the woman doctor, the immigration, the customs, and the armed guards, came a small, gray-haired man. This gray-haired man was Captain Diez, the head of the Ecuadorian Secret Police, and he was now our guest, and we had 250 cases of contraband aboard. As we shook hands, I smiled a disarming smile, and he just gave me a big, broad grin. What had the brokers in Panama radioed ahead? Would I become a permanent guest of the government?

The armed guards were not a problem. They could be bribed. But Captain Diez was an item to be reckoned with. The ship's Captain took me aside, and we had a little talk. Captain John told me to stay with Captain Diez at all times, and under no condition to let him out of my sight. I was to be with him every waking hour, and when he was asleep, too. If for any reason he found the contraband. . . I understood.

Captain Diez and I became the best of friends. I brought him coffee in the morning, sat beside him when he ate. I had the cook make him special dishes. I listened to him tell his life story, of his worldly travels, and of all the bad smugglers he had put in jail. In the warm evenings, we sat on deck sipping good Scotch whiskey, with lots of ice. I gave him a fine World Atlas. We were father and son.

Three days later we were loaded. The main engines were turning over slowly, the anchor was being hoisted, all of the guards were in the shore boat, except Captain Diez. He shook hands with our Captain, then turned to me.

Captain Diez put his hand on my shoulder and said he wished

I were his son. Would I come and live with him, in Quito, and stop working at sea? He would place me in a fine job, with the Ecuadorian Government. There was no end to what he would do for me. Captain Diez said he had never in his life been treated so fine. We put our arms around each other, and as tears came into our eyes we hugged and cried. Then he was over the side, and we were headed out to sea.

The Captain was waiting for me on the bridge. Captain John said he would nominate me for an Oscar, my acting was superb. I told him anyone would have tears in his eyes if he was clearing a port, and still had contraband aboard.

There wasn't a contraband runner in Esmeraldas, so we took the cigarettes and whiskeys back to Panama. We went dockside in Panama, and off-loaded the cargo. The owner of the cargo gave me a case of Scotch whiskey, which I divided with the crew. I have no idea what the Captain received, but I hope it was a lot more. As we sailed north, the Captain and I would sit in our overstuffed chairs on the bridge, and often talk about our bad trip to Esmeraldas, Ecuador.

The Case of Old Hook-Nose

We took on bunkers (oil) dockside in Panama, and at the same time 150 cases of Scotch whiskey, 150 cases of Lucky Strike cigarettes, and about 100 dozen women's brassieres. This "cargo" anyone may buy, for cash, out of the "free zone. " The free zone is an area where cargos are stored for transshipment. Taxation has not been placed on these cargos. Therefore, the price is very low. These cargos are purchased out of the free zone and shipped to other countries. There are free zones all over the world, a system of moving cargos from one country to another without taxation.

When we departed from Panama, our ship's agent cleared the ship and sent out our ETA (estimated time of arrival) to the next port of call. The ship's agent in this port would tell everyone from the taxi drivers to the "Aduana," when we would arrive. The Aduana is the Customs Department, and it also had common knowledge of the cargo we had on board. We would off-load this cargo to small boats, contraband runners, and they would take the cargo ashore. We were just smugglers!

We cleared Panama, setting a course south by west, for Cape San Mateo, Ecuador. Changing course to south, we had about 90 miles' run to Santa Elena Point. Our schedule was to unload the cargo about five miles offshore. The smugglers would come out in their four large dugout canoes. Each canoe powered by two 75-horsepower Johnson outboard motors.

The night was pitch black, with a warm, driving rain, as we approached Santa Elena Point. I turned on the radar, while the ship's clock rang out six bells, second dog watch, or 0300 to you land lubbers. I checked our position with the radar, turned on the fathometer, and shut off all running lights. I sent a seaman below to shut off all lights that could be seen from shore. Putting the radar on the twenty-mile range, I picked up four objects that should be the dugout canoes. I slowed the ship to half speed, then called the

Captain.

I turned the ship into the moderate swell, and as the Captain sipped his coffee, I stopped the main engine. The four large dugout canoes, with two men in each, came alongside. The men in the canoes came on board, looking like drowned rats, while part of our crew watched the canoes. Our cook was ready with hot beef sandwiches and coffee for all hands. Their leader came up to the bridge.

Lopez, the leader of the contraband runners, was a short, dark-complected Indian. His little brain was running at top speed every minute. Up on the bridge, Lopez told us that Old Hook-Nose, the head of the Aduana (Customs) was waiting for him. Old Hook-Nose had tried to catch us at our devious occupation for years. At first he told us that with a little kickback, he would look the other way. We denied everything. So now it was war!

Hook-Nose and some of the army were on shore, in the rain, waiting to catch us. I turned on the dim light in the chart room, and we looked at the coastline.

The Captain and I looked at the chart of the coastline of Ecuador, and pointed out to Lopez a fishing village. Lopez said he knew the village, and not only that, he had a cousin who lived there. If we could get him there, he could get the cargo ashore. From there, he could truck it about 75 miles to Guayaquil. As the fishing village was about 15 miles down the coast, the Captain said to pull the canoes out of the water, and we would run on down.

We unhooked the falls from a lifeboat on each side of the ship, and cranked out the davits. With a strap around the bow, and one around the stern, we hoisted up a canoe on each side. Then using more straps, rigged the same, we hoisted the second canoe on each side. Lashed tight to the side of the ship, with frapping lines, the canoes were in place. The ship's running lights were turned on, and we were full ahead.

We kept the ship in 30 fathoms, as there was a sunken wreck about five miles offshore. Daylight was breaking when Lopez pointed out the fishing village and we stopped. Lowering the canoes into the water, the cargo was stowed in them. With broad smiles, the contraband runners waved and headed for the fishing village. Setting a course for inside Santa Clara Island, we were once again underway. The Captain and I sat down to bacon and eggs, topped off with hot coffee; it had been a long night.

We turned up the easterly side of Puna Island, picked up the pilot and armed guards, then entered the Guayas River. The muddy river twists and turns for the 30 miles to Guayaquil. Slowing to dead slow. We dropped anchor off of the Molicone. The lighters, full of bananas, came alongside, and we started loading cargo.

The little shore boat came alongside, and a very tired customs officer climbed aboard. With the corners of his mouth turned down, Old Hook-Nose looked at me out of his bloodshot eyes. I gave him my ear to ear grin, and invited him into the ship's office. Hook- Nose related a fantastic story of waiting in the rain, with no lights, no fire, nothing. He had some smugglers dead to rights, this time. I asked him to stop for a minute, while I brought out a bottle of good Scotch whiskey.

As the bottle went down, the corners of his mouth went up. When I gave him a full bottle, and five cartons of cigarettes, a very tired old man smiled. Old Hook-Nose was telling me of the beautiful girls of Guayaquil, by the time the bottle was half empty. He stretched out on the couch in the ship's office, and I went out on deck to watch the loading of bananas. So ended another quiet, restful trip to Ecuador, the enchanted land of mosaic.

Sink the Louisa

We were exactly eight miles north of Santa Clara Island, Ecuador, and I had left all of our running lights on and stopped the ship. I was first officer on the Atlantic Reefer, a refrigerated cargo ship that was hauling bananas from Ecuador to gulf ports in the U. S. We had been on this run for several years and had local knowledge of the area. We would go between Santa Clara Island and Puna Island and then up into the Jambeli Channel. At the north end of Puna Island was the Puna Pilot Station, where the armed guards and the pilot came aboard.

The ship's clock struck four bells (two A. M.), and the rain poured down. Along the coast of Ecuador it rained almost every night, which is why the country produces a vast quantity of bananas. We liked the rain, because that made it miserable for the "Aduana," the Federal Customs, to find us. On our southbound trips we would bring our personal cargo of cigarettes, whiskey, handkerchiefs and women's underclothing. This illicit cargo was unloaded at sea into small boats, which would run it in to shore. The cargo was then unloaded from the small boats and sold in Guayaquil and other nearby towns. Yes, we were smugglers.

I had the fathometer and radar running and had called the Captain. The ship was in about thirty fathoms of water, and the radar showed there was a small vessel coming out to us. We had only been dealing with this organization for about six months, so we had a few weapons handy. The crew was down on the main deck standing by.

I handed a cup of coffee to John, the Captain, and we watched the small boat approach. It was George, in his thirty-foot boat, the Louisa, all right. The Louisa was tied off and our cargo was quickly loaded into it. The Ecuadorian smuggler from the small boat came aboard and we went into the office. George brought a large suitcase full of Sucres, Ecuadorian money. He knew how much we were bringing, because we had called him from Panama. If the money was close, within about a thousand dollars American, that was fine. We would receive the rest in Guayaquil.

I emptied the suitcase full of money out on the office table, and Captain John lined it up and made a fast count. John looked at George the smuggler, then said in Spanish, "You're eight thousand dollars short. " George said he didn't have the money, but he would bring it to us in Guayaquil. John told him we dealt in cash only and upon delivery. A few hundred or even up too around a thousand short was no problem, but eight thousand dollars short was a major problem.

George whined a little, telling us about how poor he was, and when he got the cargo ashore he could get the money. We had our problems, too. If we were caught with the contraband on board, the ship would be seized and we could land in jail. The cargo was loaded, so John told him to take the contraband and pay us in Guayaquil, in two days. What else could he say?

With that, George got in his launch and started up the west side of Puna Island. He had eight thousand dollars, American, of our money. Part of that money belonged to the crew, because we all shared in the contraband. George was going to have a problem.

George didn't have any lights on, but I watched him on the radar. We started the Reefer up and ran between Puna and Santa Clara Islands. With the radar and the fathometer this was easy. I remember the days we used to make this run without radar.

Daylight was breaking when we came up to the Puna pilot station. We waited and watched, and soon the pilot boat was on its way out. With the armed guards, the "Aduana," and the pilot aboard, we started up the Guayas River. It was twenty-nine miles from Puna Station to Guayaquil, and we still had the handkerchiefs to drop.

About four miles south of Guayaquil the river makes a big "S" turn. In this turn we are out of sight, only jungle on each side. Two dugout canoes with two men in each were floating there, looking for all the world like four Indians fishing. As we went by, the starboard aft loading port opened and two waterproof bundles went overboard. They were picked up by the men in the canoes, who paddled into the jungle bordering the river. We had delivered the handkerchiefs.

We anchored off Guayaquil and let out a tremendous amount of anchor chain. This is necessary because of the river current. In the spring the river can run at eight knots, so the anchor must be placed far ahead.

The paperwork was finished, and then we talked with Colonel Alban Borja, the ship's broker. There has been a Colonel Borja in Ecuador since Pizarro came here in 1539. I looked at Colonel Borja — tall, slim and gray-haired — and thought about how many generations his family had lived here. The Colonel told us the fruit was being loaded in lighters now and would arrive tomorrow morning.

John and I cleaned up and took the shore boat to the Molecon. We said hello to many of our Ecuadorian friends around the dock and walked up the few blocks to the Majestic Hotel. Fred David and his wife, Nada, managed the hotel for the Brazonie brothers, and Fred knew all of the smugglers. If Fred didn't know them personally, then he had his spies out to watch them.

We sat down with Fred and Nada, and Fred poured the Scotch on the rocks from a bottle of Chivas Regal we had smuggled in. After a little small talk, we got down to business. We told Fred about George and the eight thousand dollars. Fred smiled, held up his hands and said, in his European accent, "I know all about it. " John and I were a little surprised that our problem was common knowledge around Guayaquil.

The next morning we started loading fruit, a thirty-four-hour job. Finally, the ship was loaded and all of our refrigeration was on line, pumping the heat out of the bananas. The bananas came on board about eighty degrees, and we'd cool them to fifty-two degrees pulp temperature. We hadn't seen or heard from George.

With the pilot aboard, we hoisted the anchor and started down the river. We ran the twenty-nine miles, dropped off the pilot and headed for the open ocean. Running northbound through the Panama Canal, we cleared Colon and headed north in the Caribbean Sea. We ran up through the Yucatan Channel and into Galveston, Texas. Unloading the fruit in Galveston, we started south bound the next day. There was no word from George, and the eight thousand dollars.

We arrived in Panama five days later. Still, no word from George. We asked the ship's broker, and he said there was no word. That meant we didn't have much working capital to buy another cargo. John and I talked, along with the chief engineer, and we decided there would be no cargo this trip.

Our crew was mostly natives from around Puna Island and Guayaquil. They had all of their money in the contraband cargo, also. A good job in Guayaquil pays thirty dollars a month. We paid the seaman seventy-five dollars a month, to stop them from stealing. So when one of the crew lost two hundred dollars, which was a lot of money, the crew said they would find George.

We ran southbound through the Canal, picked up the Puna pilot and were back in Guayaquil, Ecuador. We went through the paperwork, the Colonel told us when we could expect the fruit, and then we started to look for George.

John and I went ashore and found Fred David. Fred told us that George had gone up to Quito and was not going to pay us. We went back to the ship to try and think out this problem. The ship's crew assembled on the foredeck to form a plan of action. Part of the crew had been ashore and told us the same thing that Fred had said.

As we talked, I could see we were going to have a problem with the crew. The native mind does not think like ours. They wanted revenge, and right now. They decided the money was gone, so kill George. We told them if they killed George, we'd never get any of our money back.

That night we started loading bananas in a light rain. One of the crew came up to me and told me that part of the crew had gone ashore. They were going to get some gasoline, find George's boat, the Louisa, and burn it. I told him to go find the men who were going to do this and stop them. I said to tell them that if they burned his boat, we'd never get any money.

Captain John had gone ashore to talk with Fred, and I stayed on board to watch the loading of the fruit. The hours went by. I walked around the ship, opening cargo vents and exhausting the ethylene gas that the fruit gives off, then closing the vents and telling the engineer to start the refrigeration in that particular cargo space.

About three in the morning John came back aboard. He called me into the office and closed the door. "Well, they did it," he said, sitting down in a big chair. "Fred told me they were going to burn the Louisa and there was no way I could stop them. " I sat down at the table and tried to think about what would happen now. We were both thinking. There goes our money. Just before daylight some dugout canoes came down the river and alongside. About eight of our crew climbed up the boarding ladder and disappeared into the crew's quarters.

A few hours after daylight the fruit was loaded and we called for a pilot. I made a round of the ship to see that all hands were aboard and they all greeted me with big smiling faces. I went forward and pulled the anchor and then went up to the bridge. The pilot told us about a big fire in the yacht anchorage that morning.

Again we went down the river, dropped the pilot off at Puna Island, and proceeded northbound. Arriving in Balboa, C. Z. , we were met by the boarding officers. When the paperwork was finished, the ship's broker handed John some papers. One was a letter from Fred. He must have mailed it the morning we cleared Guayaquil, to catch us in Panama.

John read the letter and then handed it to me. There were the usual salutations and then the story of the fire. As Fred told it, part of the crew went up into the jungles that border the Daule River. They acquired some dugout canoes, put some cans of gasoline in them and then floated down the Daule. The Daule is one of the two rivers merging at Guayaquil to create the Guayas River.

The crew, which was primarily Ecuadorian Indians, was in the water holding onto the canoes.

As they went by the area where George's boat was moored, they went alongside, poured the gasoline over his boat and set it on fire. Then the crew stayed in the water alongside the canoes and floated on down the river. When they were well clear, they climbed in the canoes and paddled on down to the Atlantic Reefer.

Now we were northbound in the Panama Canal. The crew was happy and we were all out eight thousand dollars. As we headed out into the Caribbean, John and I were talking about finding a new smuggler to take the contraband ashore. All this because the crew sunk the Louisa.

Illicit Cargo

We had off-loaded a cargo of fruit in San Diego, California, and my new orders were to proceed to Long Beach, California, to load general cargo bound for Mexico. I was the Captain on the Maria Inez, and we ran up and down the coast of Mexico, mostly with bananas out of Manzinillo, Mexico. My orders now were for general cargo, bound for La Paz, Baja, California.

The port pilot took us into Long Beach Harbor and we tied up starboard side to. For some reason the owners had wanted only a skeleton crew on this short trip. There would be Mexican long-shoremen to off-load the cargo. We had nothing to do with that.

Early in the morning the forward and aft hatches were opened and we were ready to load cargo. When I say general cargo, that is exactly what it was. We had farm tools and tires by the pallet. Forty tons of Gerber's baby food came aboard, along with several tons of barbed wire. We had seventeen thousand board feet of lumber and one school bus. There were ten automobiles secured on deck, along with the lumber and the bus. There were boxes of medicine and clothing, cases of canned food, and a lot of paperwork to go along with all of this.

Most of the cargo had been stored in a warehouse on the dock, some arrived as we were loading. Two days were utilized in loading the cargo. At the end of the first day I had a phone call from the owner, and it gave me one of the biggest problems of my life.

I was informed that a cargo of two thousand cases of Canadian whiskey would arrive late in the afternoon, tomorrow. This cargo was to be placed where it could be off-loaded immediately and with ease. There was to be no listing of this part of the cargo on the ship's manifest that went to the Mexican consulate. Pull this listing out of the cargo manifest — that was smuggling!

When general cargo is loaded, bound for another port, there is a record of the merchandise that is loaded. With the forty tons of Gerber's baby food, there was one sheet of paper listing all of the pertinent information. With each individual part of the general cargo, there is a listing of the items. In the end, you have forty or fifty sheets of paper which make up the cargo manifest.

To clear the ship for the high seas, this cargo manifest is presented to the American authorities. They keep a copy and authorize the clearance of the vessel. You then take the cargo manifest to the consulate of the country for which you are bound. In my case, I was bound for La Paz, Mexico, so I went to the Mexican consulate. By extracting the sheet of paper that listed the Canadian whiskey, not declaring it, I then had to land the whiskey surreptitiously. The Mexican Consulate would stamp the manifest, keeping a copy, also. You were now cleared for Mexico.

This is exactly what I did. I cleared the ship with the U. S. authorities, then pulled the whiskey listing out of the ship's manifest and cleared the ship with the Mexican government.

I didn't like the idea of carrying two thousand cases of Canadian whiskey to be smuggled into Mexico. I didn't know the people who were to unload it, and I didn't know their boat. I knew nothing of the operation, only that I had the cargo, and if I were caught I would be the one to go to jail. That I was told on the telephone was a bad sign. It was unwise to discuss an operation like this over the phone. I was dealing with rank amateurs. I talked with John Radine, who was sailing with me as first officer, and we decided to take the ship to Mexico — make the run!

In the late afternoon of the second day, when the general cargo had been loaded, a very large truck came alongside the forward loading hatch. The doors were sealed, and a U. S. Customs officer broke the seal and opened the loading doors. The whiskey had arrived from Canada in bond — without paying U. S. tax.

The longshoremen started loading pallets, and the whiskey was swung aboard with the "schooner gear. " I was standing with the U. S. Customs agent, at the edge of the pier, when an empty wooden whiskey case floated by on the flood tide. The agent immediately went to a telephone and called the Federal Bureau of Investigation, Long Beach. I walked aboard the Maria Inez and told the hatch tender to tell the men below that they'd better be "clean" when they came off of the ship.

Two carloads of F. B. I. men arrived within minutes. They stood by the gangplank. As the men came off of the ship, they were searched. One man complained of the search, and was immediately arrested and whisked away to jail.

The cargo was loaded, and I cleared the ship with the United States authorities, and also with the Mexican Consulate. The pilot came aboard, we cleared Long Beach Harbor for the high seas, and I set a course for the Coronado Islands. But our problems were not over, not by a long shot.

I had known John Radine for a long, long time. When I was a kid in high school, I used to wrestle with him on the front lawn of his house in San Pedro. I had sailed several years with John, when he was Captain of the Atlantic Reefer. John was a relative and long time employee of the ship's owner. As we cleared Long Beach, John came up on the bridge.

John leaned on the engine room telegraph and said, "You don't know this, but we have to go inside the Coronados and pick up a small barge. "

"I was wondering how we were going to unload this whiskey. Of course you know we're smuggling into Mexico, and the whole business stinks!" I spit back at him. It was about a ninety-mile run; we would arrive at the Mexican border just after daylight.

Part of the crew came up on the bridge, and we all talked about smuggling the whiskey. Up until now, John and I were the only ones who knew we were smuggling. The rest of the crew was aboard just to run the ship. Now they were asking what would happen if we were caught, how long a jail term do you get in Mexico and if they would go to jail. I told them I didn't think the crew would be responsible, only the Captain, and Mexico had a penal colony - Tres Marias Islands.

The day broke calm and clear, John and I were both on the

bridge. We were not up to the Coronados, so we were still in U. S. waters, but very close to the border. Just outside the sea buoy, at the entrance to San Diego Harbor, we saw a small work boat towing a blunt-nosed barge. We drifted along, and the work boat caught up with us. We took the barge from the work boat, secured it and very slowly got underway.

John had all of the information about the landing of the whiskey and now he told me, "I've never known a plan, if you want to call it a plan, as bad as this. This plan is something that someone must have read in some old pirate story. It's not going to work. "

The plan was this. We'd take the little barge and run outside the Coronado Islands. Then under the cover of darkness we'd come back to the shoreline at Descanso Point. We would look for a blinking green light, that would be the smugglers. They would come out in a small boat, and then we'd load the whiskey into the little barge, and they'd take the load ashore. The little barge would hold about five hundred cases, so it would have to make four trips.

This plan, without a doubt, was the worst idea I had ever heard of. To begin with, you had the Mexican police patrolling the highway. Second you had to either constantly maneuver the ship or drop the anchor. If you dropped the anchor and a coast patrol boat came up, what did you say? Third, that was a rock-bound coast, and if we got in close, there could be submerged rocks. The sun went down and we turned the Maria Inez toward shore.

We came into the land about three miles south of the border and turned down the coast. With no running lights, all lights out and the dead lights secured, we ran into six fathoms of water. I checked the tide table twice, and we were almost at a high tide. On a chart, the soundings are marked at a low tide, we had a fathometer running, showing us the water below the ship's keel. The night was black, which was a great help.

John had a terrible cold along with a bad cough, and as the night wore on, he was miserable. We were both out on the port wing of the ship, scanning the shoreline for a green light. There

123

was no light, except for the headlights of cars on the Mexican freeway. I watched the navigation of the ship and John concentrated on finding a green light. There was nothing!

We ran at about eight knots along the coast, in six fathoms of water. I pulled out a little at Point Descanso, because of submerged rocks, and then back into six fathoms. The ship stayed in six fathoms around Salsipuedes Point and still no green light. When we arrived at Point San Miguel, I changed course and ran back up the coast.

By now there weren't so many headlights. The night air was cold, and we were running in five fathoms. We took the ship up past the lights of Rosarito Beach and even with the Coronado Islands. The time was four in the morning and we were tired. We had run the coast twice, and in five fathoms of water, or thirty feet below the keel. This was crazy. John and I decided we would run out to sea twenty or thirty miles, so we came up to full speed.

We ran westerly, offshore, till daylight and then slowed down. Turning on the transmitter for the radio, we called our principals. In plain language we told them we were having engine trouble, and they would have to fly some small parts down to us. We told them we could get the ship to San Quintin Bay, but they would have to meet us with the parts.

They understood, and we gave them some small part numbers for one of the main generators. They told us to try to get the engine running one more time, and they could meet us with the parts tomorrow afternoon. We understood this to mean for us to make one more pass from Rosarito to Descanso. Our principals knew the speed of the ship, so they knew the run to San Quintin would take ten hours. When they told us they would fly in the parts in the afternoon, we understood them to say for us to make the pass ten hours earlier. This meant for us to run the coast about three o'clock in the morning.

We drifted most of the day, did a little fishing, and around midnight we started up the Maria Inez. We arrived just north of Rosarito Beach, and headed down the coast in five fathoms under the keel. Traveling at about eight knots, we scrutinized the coast, but there was no green light. Upon reaching Descanso Point, we brought the ship up to speed and headed offshore. We were well out to sea by daylight. When we were about twenty miles offshore, I changed course for San Quintin Bay. John and I went to bed, and let the deck watch handle the bridge. We would arrive in San Quintin shortly after noon.

We brought the Maria Inez into San Quintin Bay, under a pretext of engine trouble. It was a beautiful, sunny day, with calm seas, so we lay there with nothing to do, just waiting. We had a little sixteen-foot skiff that was very light and strong. There was a seventy-five-horsepower outboard motor to go on it. One of the crew, Bob Martinolich, wanted to go fishing, and as we were going to use the little skiff for transportation to the beach, I said certainly. We put the skiff in the water, then handed down the big motor and fishing gear. Bob, in the stern of the little boat, was ready to start the motor.

Alone in the skiff, Bob pulled the cord to start the motor. It fired the first pull, and with a roar, the bow of the skiff came up out of the water. The stern, with the motor, went down. Bob jumped to the bow to hold it down with his weight, and away they went across San Quintin Bay.

All of us watched him skimming over the water, Bob holding down the bow, and the seventy-five-horsepower motor at a full throttle. Bob would try to get back to the stern to shut the engine off, but each time the bow of the skiff rose up, high out of the water. It didn't take long for Bob to learn to shift his weight, and by this means to steer the boat.

I could see that when he jumped to the stern to stop the motor, the bow came up. I also understood that if and when he did stop the motor, the boat would swamp and we could lose the motor. I had part of the crew with heaving lines and some others in bathing suits standing by.

Bob came by close to the port side of the Maria Inez, jumped to the stern and cut the motor. The boat swamped. The heaving lines were thrown out, and the men in bathing suits dove overboard and attached the heaving lines to the motor and boat. We pulled the boat and motor aboard, and the chief engineer immediately went to work on the motor. In a short time the motor was running again, and we were ready for visitors. No question about it, Bob had a spectacular ride.

By the time we had a cup of coffee, a single engine airplane buzzed us and headed toward land. John knew the plane and went ashore to pick up our principals. John brought back three Mexicans. They were right out of television. All three looked like something out of a George Raft picture, only they didn't flip the coin.

We went into the galley, all talking at once. They said we were so close to them they could almost touch us, why didn't we see the green light? They were on the bluff just a mile north of Rosarito Beach. They had a green filter over a three-cell flashlight. A flashlight! We told them the headlights of a car were bad enough, but a little flashlight! We were dealing with amateurs.

We had to take the ship to La Paz because of the general cargo, but we didn't want to take the whiskey into that port. We were told to unload the whiskey on Cerralvo Island first, then proceed to La Paz. Cerralvo, just up from the Cape and before La Paz, is uninhabited, with a sandy beach on the south end.

If we made it out of La Paz after unloading our general cargo, we would then stop at Cerralvo Island, and load the whiskey back on aboard. Then, with the whiskey on board, we would go back around the cape and up to Rosarito. Just a mile north of Rosarito is a small cove with a sandy beach. We would unload the two thousand cases of Canadian whiskey there.

We were back out to sea and I set a course for well outside Cedros Island. I brought two cups of coffee up to the bridge, and John and I sat down to have a long talk. We knew by now we were dealing with a bunch of clowns. They had been watching television too long. Unloading the whiskey on Ceralvo Island was the worst scenario imaginable. It would take hours and hours. We decided we would do the job our way.

We arrived at Cerralvo Island about sundown, pulled into shallow water and dropped the anchor. We were all going to have a good sleep, then hide the whiskey on board the Maria Inez. There would be no off-loading on Cerralvo Island.

On the Maria Inez there was a small cargo hold that was situated the next deck above the fuel oil tanks. There was a small hatch from the deck above, and a large door from the forward cargo hold. These were the only access to this area, almost a void. This void was situated from the upper engine room bulkhead, forward about twenty feet, where it terminated with another bulkhead. This area would hold two thousand cases of whiskey and a little more. We moved the whiskey into this void, closed the bulkhead door and stacked all types of dunnage and equipment in front of it.

While we were hoisting the anchor, just after daylight, a Mexican army airplane flew over us. This plane, an old "Texan" trainer from United States, made two passes over us about two hundred feet up. At this time, we knew the Mexican Government was onto us. Someone had told them about the contraband.

Now we had a major problem. Should we throw the whiskey overboard, or try to take it in and out of La Paz? John and I debated for a half an hour. We decided to take the contraband into La Paz, and get it back out again. If we failed, we'd both go to Tres Maria Islands.

With this in mind, we went up the west side of Cerralvo Island to Coyote Point. Turning west, we ran through the narrow channel and were in La Paz Bay. With our flags up and the pilot on board, we went dockside. The port officials came aboard, the doctor, then the Immigration and Customs. They all went ashore, except the Customs. There were a lot of Customs officers, more than normal. This was a search party!

The Customs official, or "Aduana," read each paper of the ship's manifest. John was on his left and I was on his right, but John was thinking faster than I. As the Customs man turned over one sheet of paper, John reached out and grabbed the next paper on the pile. Crumpling the paper up in his hand, John told the official that the paper was no good. It was from a previous trip. Surprisingly enough, the Customs official bought this explanation. The paper was a list of the whiskey we had on board. I had missed it when I took out the whiskey manifest. Close!

With the paperwork finished, the big search was on. We were now playing cat and mouse, except for big stakes. We covered the ship. They were looking for a large area, and I was smiling and talking as fast as I could. Finally we went down into the engine room. They searched the lower engine room, and coming up the ladder at the forward end of the engine room, asked me what was on the other side of the bulkhead. When in the lower engine room, I told them the ship's fuel tanks. We stood on the upper engine room deck and I told them the forward cargo hold. Actually it was the void with the whiskey. They stood there and thought for a while, then on with the search.

We went up to the main deck, and walked the twenty feet to the forward cargo hold. Going down alongside a bulkhead, they asked me what was on the other side. I told them the engine room! We went from the cargo hold, twenty feet to the engine room and each time I told them it was the "...other side of the bulkhead. " I excelled as a Spanish orator that day.

There is one thing I know for a fact. From the United States to the end of South America, when you ask a man about their women, his mind stops cold. He cannot remember what he was talking about. This is the only thing that saved us. As we walked the twenty feet, I would stop and ask how sexy were the beautiful women in this port. The Aduana would stop, turn toward me, and give me a long speech about the women. At this point he had forgotten how many feet he had walked, and maybe he didn't care. I know this much, when I mentioned the women, the Aduana stopped, his mind a blank. We were finally cleared for entry.

Within a few hours we started off-loading the cargo, and everything ran smoothly. The automobiles and school bus were first, then the lumber, then into the cargo holds. We would probably be unloaded in two days. There was no night shift.

Our principals flew in, and we all had dinner in the hotel. Not a word was said about their whiskey. They came aboard the ship for a half an hour, and then flew back to San Diego. We now understood what they wanted.

About midnight the Aduana returned to the ship. I was awakened and went down to the galley. There was a search party again. Once again John and I went around with the search party, but there was nothing they could find. Reluctantly, they abandoned the search about two in the morning.

The cargo was unloaded, the pilot was aboard, and our little barge was still in tow, as we headed out of La Paz. It was dark when we left the dock, and took the short cut around Coyote Point. We ran down the west side of Cerralvo Island, turned east and were clear of land in an hour. A few more hours, and by daylight we were in the open ocean, headed up the coast. Next stop Rosarito Beach.

After running along the coast for two days, we arrived at our destination, the little cove with the sandy beach, just north of Rosarito Beach. John and I looked ashore. There was no doubt this was the right place. There was a big bulldozer, which had cut a wide road down to the beach, along with three or four large trucks. About twenty men were waving at us, so we pulled in close to shore, and dropped the anchor in broad daylight.

We had a work boat on deck, so we put that in the water and loaded it with cases of whiskey. When the work boat left, we pulled the little barge alongside, and loaded about seven hundred cases in it. The work boat towed the barge into shore, and anchored it just outside the surf line, then came back for another load.

Our work boat made three trips into shore, and the barge was anchored close to shore. As the work boat pulled out with the third and last load, we were hoisting the anchor. When the work boat came alongside, we hooked onto it and started hoisting it aboard.

As the little boat cleared the water, I stepped back into the pilot house and put the ship to full speed ahead. We had just smuggled two thousand cases of Canadian whiskey!

There were two Americans fishing off of the rocks overlooking the beach. Tony, the man in charge of the smugglers, put two of his gunmen behind the Americans, telling them they would be shot if they left before the operation was finished. The Americans watched everything. I often wonder what they were thinking.

Later, a friend of mine who had a lobster business in the same area, told me a strange story. My friend had gone into the shack of his lobster supplier, on top of the bluff, and there were cases of Canadian whiskey. His Mexican partner said a ship named the Maria Inez had unloaded a lot of cases of whiskey. There had been a barge full of whiskey anchored close to shore. During the night the barge sank, and the next day there were men skindiving for cases of whiskey. When the divers were gone, he dove down and found eight more cases. Have a drink!

In the weeks to come, one of the crewmen of this ignoble voyage made a Saturday afternoon trip to Tijuana, for some fun and frolic. As he sauntered down the main street, two big, black limousines pulled up beside him. Two large Mexicans jumped out, grabbed him, and shoved him into one of the limos. When he looked up, he found he was seated between two men with submachine guns. Tony, the head smuggler, smiled at him and told him not to be afraid, he was under their protection!

The crewman came back to San Diego as fast as he could. For many, many years to come, no person who had been on that voyage went to Mexico. I continued on the banana run to Manzinillo, Mexico, but with a different crew.

How did the Aduana know we had the whiskey? Well, apparently, a competitor in a small shipping company, someone with a deceivious mind, had looked at our ship's manifest. The one left with the American authorities. He then went to the Mexican consulate, looked at the ship's manifest, and knew we were "running" the whiskey. To eliminate the competition, he informed the

Mexican Customs. Our principals notified the Mexican smugglers, and that's all I know of that.

This voyage was undoubtedly the worst trip of my life. The trip was ill-planned, poorly executed, with extreme jeopardy to all concerned. John and I finally saved the "cargo," but just barely. Truly an illicit cargo.

Hot Cargo

The Atlantic Reefer, a refrigerated cargo ship, was tied up at pier two in Miami, Florida. Captain John Radine was in command, while I was second in command. My job covered communications, navigation, cargo storage and just about anything else. I was kind of like the "girl Friday" in the office…you know, make the coffee, take out the trash, sweep the floor, do all of the office work and laugh at the boss's bad jokes.

Captain John told me to go to the shipyard and pick up something for the engine room. I took the company rental truck and drove to the shipyard, across from the Robert Clay pool, on the Miami river. I asked the cute little blonde secretary for the item and she gave it to me. She asked me a few questions about the Reefer, then to my surprise asked if she could come over for a cup of coffee. I said, "Certainly. Be glad to show you around. " Then I asked if she'd like to have lunch today. She said that would be great.

The ship's officers ate in one area and the rest of the crew had their own mess room. After lunch the engineers went back to work down below, and John and I showed her around the ship. She was friendly, and certainly not the dumb blonde she let on to be. In fact, she was a lot smarter than was necessary, just to be working in the shipyard as a typist or whatever.

We were on the bridge when she turned to John, and asked if he had ever smuggled anything. John said yes, we had been known to bring in a few items, why? She said that she was the contact for an organization that supplied whiskey to the east coast. Well!

I sat on the chart table, John leaned against the engine room telegraph and she said, just as casual as could be, "I know some people who would like you to bring them a few thousand cases of whiskey. "

I looked at John, he looked at me, and we both blinked. We had never, in our fondest dreams, thought of bringing an illicit cargo into the United States. That is a no-no! We would take cigarettes and whiskey into South America, because that is how business operated in South America, but under no circumstances into the U. S. First, this was where we lived — it was our home. Secondly, you didn't bribe a U. S. Customs agent. Maybe the big politicians, but not the American working man.

John said, "Well, I don't know. I guess I could talk to your principals. "

The little blonde smiled sweetly and said, "I'll make a phone call and be right back. "

She was back in about a half hour, marched onboard and went straight to John. After having a few words with John, the little blonde walked off of the ship and down the pier. I went over to John, being curious, and asked what she said. John smiled and said, "I'll pick her up outside the shipyard, and we'll have a drink at the bar in the Alcazar Hotel, there on Biscayne Boulevard. "

In the late afternoon John walked aboard and called me into the office. We sat down and John said, "These people supply the east coast with whiskey. They want us to bring in five thousand cases. They tell me that half of the whiskey on the east coast is brought in illegally. "

"Five thousand cases!" I exclaimed. "That's a boxcar full. Forget it John, that's out of our league. "

John was silent for a long time, then looked at me and said, "What if we had, say, a thousand cases and put them on a boat offshore ten or twenty miles, say, halfway to Havana?"

"They're bringing shiploads of whiskey out of the free port on Martinique Island, but these are the big boys. I want nothing to do with it. " I made myself clear on this point. A little pocket money for a few seamen was one thing, but to be involved in a big operation was out of the question, as far as I was concerned.

John let the matter drop with this little talk. Two days later we cleared Miami and were on our way to Panama. Passing through the canal, southbound, we proceeded to Guayaquil, Ecuador.

We had our usual personal `business cargo,' which we

133

unloaded, and then loaded fruit. With a full load of bananas, we headed for Panama, northbound. We arrived in the Canal Zone about sundown and went dockside.

We were taking on fuel and fresh water when a large van pulled up. I talked to the driver, and he said he had fifty cases of Scotch whiskey for us. I told him to wait a minute. I'd call the Captain. I called John and he said yes, he had ordered the fifty cases. The Captain was up to something, and he hadn't told me. That was strange.

We loaded the fifty cases of whiskey on deck, John signed for it, then the two of us went into the office. Somehow I was going to be involved in this, and I didn't like it.

The weather was fair, a few whitecaps and a rolling sea from the east. Clearing Panama, I had set a course for Providence Island. John and I were on the bridge, relaxing in our large chairs. We had one big chair on each side of the bridge. With coffee in hand, John told me what he had agreed to.

John had made a deal to bring fifty cases of Scotch whiskey from the free zone in Panama, and meet a large motor yacht off of the coast of Florida. As the weather was good, the fifty cases were secured on the lower deck, lee side.

We passed east of Old Providence Island, west of Quita Sueno Bank and on course for the west end of Cuba — Cape San Antonio. Rounding Cape San Antonio, I let the ship run offshore into deep water and set a course for Miami, Florida.

John told me to set a course for twenty miles off Alligator Key Light. This light has a range of about twenty-two miles, and you can see the flash on the clouds at thirty miles. This is where a small boat was to meet us, and unload the whiskey. We would be in the Straits of Florida, which are the shipping lanes. There are a lot of tankers that bring oil out of the Gulf ports, bound for the East Coast, and this is their route.

We were scheduled to pass through this area about 0200 on this dark night. Captain Radine said this was a trial run, just to see what these people could do. Did they have a boat, would they be on time, were they reliable? This is what John wanted to know. If they knew what they were doing, then John might work along with them.

I was on the bridge at 0100 with a cup of black coffee and two seamen. In a short while I saw the flash of light on the clouds, counted the seconds between the flashes of light and identified the light. We were on schedule and in the right place. I turned on the radar. There were several large vessels moving along the shipping lane, but I couldn't see any small return on the radar.

One large vessel was ahead of us, northbound, and we passed another on our port side, southbound. There were no other vessels on the radar. All of our running lights were on, and so were the lower deck lights, we were lit up like a Christmas tree. I checked the radar, took another look at the horizon and called the Captain.

John came up to the bridge. A seaman brought coffee for all of us, and all eyes were searching the horizon. We let the ship run in a little closer and watched the radar. The radar could pick up a small skiff in the water, and would certainly pick up a fifty-foot boat. There was nothing in sight, only that large northbound ship. Adjusting the radar to the forty-mile range, I saw that we were where we should be, twenty miles off Alligator light. It looked like we had a no show organization, there was no boat to meet us, no place to unload the whiskey. John had a problem!

The Government printed a little book, called H. O. 117. It is a table of distances from any port in the world to any other port in the world. Some bookkeeper in the company office always has a copy, and this is how they check your time of arrival. For this reason, a ship cannot stop for a few hours, or you're off schedule.

We took a last look around, with radar and visual, and were back on course for Miami, Florida. John was quite upset. It was his fifty cases, his money. After talking for a short while, John said to hide the fifty cases and we would take them into Miami. John told me to put them in the upper engine room. There was an exceptionally large lube oil tank on the upper engine room deck, that had all of the baffles cut out, and it was clean inside. The sounding pipe had a plate welded on the bottom and we kept the pipe full of lube oil. If a search party sounded the tank, it looked like it was full of lube oil.

As we were now in the shipping lanes, John stayed on the bridge while I went below and talked with the engineer. I had sailed with the engineer several years before, and he was a good man. The engineer and I carried the fifty cases down the ladder and across the upper engine room to the big lube oil tank. I pulled off the inspection plate, and case by case I placed the whiskey in the tank.

The upper engine room was warm, but inside the tank the temperature was way more than a hundred degrees. At long last I had the fifty cases of whiskey in the lube oil tank, and bolted down the inspection plate. I went to a forward cargo hold and picked off four or five green bananas. Going back down into the engine room, I rubbed the banana skin on the inspection plate. The latex in bananas ages paint immediately. In a few minutes the plate looked like it hadn't been disturbed for years and years. It was after daylight when I went up to the bridge and talked to John.

We picked up the pilot at the entrance to Miami, Florida, and he gave us his usual lecture on how to eat hominy grits. Put the grits on a plate, and then put two or three eggs over the grits. If you don't eat them that way, then you're a Damned Yankee. He took us to pier two and we started unloading immediately. In about an hour, a barge came alongside and started pumping on diesel fuel. By the time the bananas were unloaded we were fueled, and with pilot aboard, we headed out to sea.

I set a course for the west end of Cuba, then John and I sat down to talk. We still had the fifty cases of whiskey in the lube oil tank. John said to leave them there, and we would load fruit in Ecuador, then return to the States in about three weeks. On the next trip we were scheduled to stay in port for a week, and make major repairs on the main generators. During this time we would unload the whiskey.

The trip was routine, southbound through the Canal, load fruit in Guayaquil and then head north again. We rolled north across the Caribbean, around Cuba, and finally had the pilot aboard at Miami. We moored at pier two and discharged cargo. The next day all was quiet. John came aboard and said we would move the ship to the little shipyard on the Miami River. From beginning to end, we should have never gone to the little shipyard. We were four and five-foot in the mud, because of our draft. But at last we moored the ship at the dock. Once again all was quiet. John said to take out the whiskey, ready to load onto a truck.

Pappy Tucker, the chief engineer, and I went below to open up the lube oil tank. When the inspection plate was off, the smell of whiskey filled the engine room. In these wooden cases of scotch whiskey, the bottles were packed in straw, laying on their side, not upright. With the extended time in the tank, and the temperature more than a hundred degrees, all of the bottles had blown out their corks. The bottles were only half full, the other half was saturated in the straw and sloshing in the bottom of the fuel tank.

There was no way to breathe in the tank. The engine room was bad enough, so we took an air hose from the ship's air tank, and blew fresh air into the oil tank. Even with the fresh air blowing into the tank, it was impossible to breathe. I had a face mask, used for diving under water, so I ran up to my room and pulled it out. With the air hose hooked up to my face mask, I entered the tank. On my hands and knees in sloshing whiskey, I passed the half full cases out of the tank to Pappy.

By now the smell in the engine room was so bad, it was hard to breathe. Pappy started all of the big exhaust blowers for the engine room. Cubic yards of fresh air poured in, but cubic yards of whiskey-smelling air were pumped out, too. Through a hatch in the aft bulkhead, we moved the cases into a cargo hold. As the whiskey bottles were only half full, we started pouring the contents of one bottle into another. At last we had about twenty cases of bottled Scotch whiskey. By this time, Pappy and I were both about half drunk on the fumes alone.

We staggered out on deck to get some fresh air, and clear our heads. I didn't believe you could get drunk just on the smell, but believe me, you can. As we leaned against the railing, a fisherman came walking along the dock. He stopped alongside, and looking up at us, said, "Boy, that really smells good. I've been fishing along the river and you can smell that paint all the way to the bay."

"Yeah," the chief said, "we're painting the engine room and that alcohol-base paint is so bad we had to get out for a while. " The fisherman said he was retired Navy, and knew all about the quick-drying alcohol-base paint.

In a few hours a little truck pulled up to the ship, and we loaded the twenty cases of whiskey on it. With a tarp over the top, the truck drove out of the shipyard. Pappy and I sat down for a cup of fresh coffee. We had just completed the most miserable job we could think of. We could now relax!

About sundown the same little truck, with the tarp over the cases of whiskey, pulled back alongside. The driver told us the principals didn't want the whiskey, as it smelled like fuel oil. I looked at him and said, "You can have it for ten dollars a case. Just get it out of here. " The truck merrily bounced out of the yard and this time we were finished with it.

The next day John came aboard and asked how everything went. We told him the story and then told him we gave the whiskey away for ten dollars a case. John looked at us, then quietly went up to his room and closed the door. He was not a happy man. The chief and I went back in the galley for another cup of coffee.

During the following few days we surreptitiously destroyed the remaining straw and wooden cases. The work in the engine room was finished, and with a tugboat alongside, we were backed down the Miami river and into Biscayne Bay. With the pilot aboard, we headed out the channel to the open ocean. Clearing the outer sea buoy, once again I set a course for the west end of Cuba. With a cup of coffee in hand, John and I looked out the windows of the bridge and talked.

John paid twenty-five dollars a case for good Scotch whiskey.

John paid twenty-five dollars a case for good Scotch whiskey. That amounted to one thousand, two hundred and fifty dollars. I sold the twenty cases for ten dollars each, amounting to two hundred dollars. John had just lost one thousand and fifty dollars, not to mention all of our work and the risk to the ship.

John learned a good lesson — don't try to smuggle into the United States. And we all learned another lesson — don't carry bottles with corks in the lube oil tank for a long time. If you do, believe me, you will have a really "hot" cargo.

Bolts of Silk

The M. V. Atlantic Reefer was moored dockside in the Panama Canal Zone. I stood at the chart table poring over a chart of the Caribbean, dreaming of the pirates in the old days, when the Captain, John Radine, walked in. "Well, what's up?" I asked, as it started to rain outside.

"I have a new idea, something we haven't done in the past," John answered. He looked out the open door at the raindrops hitting the deck, and turning around, he said, "This trip I have eighty bolts of silk to take to Ecuador. "

I was first mate on the Atlantic Reefer. We were employed by the West Indies Fruit Company to haul bananas from Ecuador to Miami, Florida. On the southbound trips we would take cigarettes, whiskey, handkerchiefs and women's undergarments as our personal cargo to smuggle into Ecuador. Our contacts were very reliable, and would meet the ship out at sea. They, in turn, would carry the goods into shore, load it on trucks and take it into Guayaquil, Ecuador.

There is a law in Ecuador that no silk may be brought into the country in any shape or form. You cannot bring in women's clothing by paying the duty, yet all of the wealthy women wear silk dresses. There is not a ready-made dress shop in Guayaquil. All dresses are handmade. I never gave this any thought, until John started talking about the bolts of silk. The idea slowly dawned on me. Someone was smuggling in bolts of silk, so why not us? The warm rain poured down, John and I went below for a cup of coffee.

As luck would have it, the rain stopped as a truck pulled alongside the ship. We loaded the eighty bolts of silk, along with the usual cigarettes, whiskey and handkerchiefs, into the forward hold of the ship. About sundown we had finished taking on fuel and water, and with the pilot aboard, we cleared the dock and

The trip from Panama to Ecuador was pleasant, with a slight rolling sea from the west. Then we approached Point Santa Elena, on the southern coast of Ecuador. The position where we were to meet the launch from shore, was ten miles due west of Point Santa Elena, about the hundred fathom curve line. We used to go in closer to shore, but now we stayed outside the hundred fathom curve.

The weather was fine, no rain and clear as a bell. We arrived on station just after midnight, and I called the Captain. I had the radar and fathometer on, and could see a return on the radar that looked like a small boat, there was nothing else. We left all of our running light on, and all lights on the lower deck. There was no doubt we were here.

The launch came alongside, was tied off, and our crew started loading it with our cargo. The crew of the launch came aboard for a hot dinner and coffee, while their head man, Lopez, paid us for the goods. We were paid in the old worn-out Ecuadorian money, the Sucre. There is never time to count the money, you just looked at it and made a guess. Any difference, we would address in Guayaquil. Lopez could be trusted, and his launch was big enough to carry a large cargo. We watched the silk go ashore.

We brought the ship up to speed, and I set a south-east course for the end of Puna Island. Arriving at the Puna Pilot station at about 1100, we picked up the pilot and armed guard. The twenty-nine miles up the Guayas River was covered in a little over two hours, and we anchored off the Malecon at Guayaquil, Ecuador.

We went through the formality of paperwork, and passing out the cigarettes and whiskey to all of the authorities, then they were gone. Our agent, Colonel Alban Borja, told us we would start loading bananas first thing in the morning. John and I cleaned up and went ashore, to meet Lopez at the Majestic Hotel. We finalized our business transaction with Lopez, had dinner with Fred and Nada, then went back to the ship. We stretched out in our bunks and were soon fast asleep. It had been a long day.

At daylight the steel barges, laden with green fruit, were brought alongside, and we started loading bananas. John was engaged with something, and I was watching the loading of the fruit, when the shore boat came alongside. Three very tall, slim and well-dressed Ecuadorian businessmen stepped onto the deck. These were not the average businessmen, and I was apprehensive.

I greeted them, led them to our little ship's office, then called John. These men spoke excellent English, and were evidently educated in the United States. We sat in the office and made small talk for about ten minutes, then got down to business. The men introduced themselves and we had a surprise, a shock. One was the Minister of the Interior, another was the Minister of the Navy, and the third was Minister of something else. This was the Ecuadorian government!

These three men were extremely polite and courteous. As we talked, they explained the situation. In past years, these men had been instrumental in passing the law that no silk could be brought into Ecuador in any form. These three men had the silk business, they brought in the silk. They had a private beach, guarded by the Navy. They had the organization, and they were the only ones who could smuggle in the silk. The Government was in the smuggling business!

The Minister of the Navy said if we brought another load of silk into Ecuador, he would have one of the Ecuadorian gunboats come out and sink the Atlantic Reefer. That was final. The Minister of the Interior told us we could bring in all of the cigarettes, whiskey and women's underclothes that we wished, but not one bolt of silk or any silk dresses.

As John and I sat there, we learned a great lesson in the politics of the Ecuadorian Government. These high government officials had the silk smuggling business, and made no bones about it. They had the power to sink the Atlantic Reefer, and they held the power of life and death.

With a full load of fruit, we ran down the Guayas River and out to the open ocean. In the open ocean, where John and I could talk, we decided to get out of the silk smuggling business, forever.

Fred David

The Atlantic Reefer, a small refrigerated cargo ship, was moored at pier 22 in Galveston, Texas. Captain John Radine was in command, and I was next. I was in the pilot house when John walked in and said, "I have some good news. I'm going to take this trip off and go home, so you're the Captain. "

"Great," I said. "I'm glad you can get a few weeks off to go home. " I had a Master's License that covered this ship, and I was the navigator-radioman anyhow.

The next morning John was on his way home to San Pedro, California, and with pilot aboard, I was on my way to the outer sea buoy and on to Ecuador. We ran the five days to Panama and made the southbound transit of the Canal. Then another three days and we were at the mouth of the Jambeli River, in southern Ecuador. I took the ship up the river to Puerto Bolivar and dropped the anchor. The cargo holds were pre-cooled and we were ready to load fruit. I spent the evening in Machala, at a private club for plantation owners, then returned to the ship that night. Tomorrow we would start loading fruit.

The next day I was up bright and early, and the fruit was coming alongside. In this operation we anchored in a river, and then barges, or lighters as they are called, were brought alongside, loaded with green bananas. The fruit was then carried up a ramp and placed in the elevator, to disappear into the depths of the ship.

Down in the prechilled cargo holds, the men would stack two upright and then place one stem on top, flat. We could carry twenty thousand stems.

I spent the day watching the cargo come aboard and working with the refrigeration engineer. As a cargo space is filled with green fruit, whose temperature is about eighty-eight degrees, it is closed off and then the air, with ethylene gas, is extracted. Clean air replaces it. Then the cold air is blown over the hot fruit, taking the heat out of the fruit. This continues until the temperature of the fruit is fifty-two degrees. If the fruit is cooled to a lower tempera-

143

ture, it is called "chilled" fruit; the latex in the skin freezes, and the fruit will turn black. Who wants a black banana?

As the wolves of night chased the chariot of the sun into the western ocean, darkness descended upon us. Floodlights were turned on, and the big generator on shore was started, so there were lights in Puerto Bolivar. The hundred-and-twenty-pound stems of bananas slowly filled the cargo holds, and a light drizzle cooled the air.

I was watching the loading operation on the starboard side, when one of the crew came up to me and said that a canoe, with two white people, had come along the off side. I went to the ladder on the port side and there, to my delight, stood Nada and Fred David.

Nada, the fiery redheaded music teacher, and Fred, the linguistic marvel who spoke seventeen languages fluently, went back a long time. I had known Nada (Foster) in Miami, Florida, and at the same time I knew Fred and his Russian wife (who had just passed away from cancer) in Guayaquil, Ecuador. Nada had moved to Guayaquil, met Fred, fell in love and they were married.

Nada was an American citizen and Fred . . . well, Fred didn't have a country. Fred was one of those people who didn't have a country to be buried in. Because Fred was married to an American citizen, he had a priority status for American citizenship. Now they were on board the Atlantic Reefer, I was the Captain, and they wanted me to take them to the United States. I looked at their paperwork, consisting of letters from the American Embassy in Quito, Ecuador, and everything looked good to me. I loved them both dearly. With a big smile, I said, "You bet. I'll take you to the U. S. "

Fred David was a great hero, one of those men you never hear about, but he helped to make us free. Fred was born in Budapest, Hungary, about the turn of the century. With the disruption of the Habsburg, German and Russian Empires, which led to war in 1914, new countries were made and old countries obliterated. When the smoke cleared away, Fred was a Russian captive, working in the Siberian salt mines, with no identification. When the American Expeditionary force went into Europe in World War One, somehow Fred was set free.

Fred became a train conductor on the Trans-Siberian Railway or one that ran to Mongolia. One day, he and his White Russian wife stepped off of the train, and started walking into Mongolia. They lived with a Mongolian warlord for a short time. One day the warlord had one thousand Chinese beheaded. The warlord asked Fred if he would give the signal. Fred said yes and raised his arm. When Fred brought his arm down, the heads were cut off of a thousand men. The men were in a line, as far as Fred could see. After beheading a thousand Chinese, Fred and his Russian wife walked on across the Gobi desert, and ended up in Shanghai, China. By this time Fred spoke Hungarian, Russian, several dialects of Chinese. He learned French and English, as the fore-man of the French-American Tobacco Company in Shanghai.

When the Japanese bombed Shanghai, and the war started in China, Fred and his wife moved to a nice quiet island in the Philippines. Fred set up a rice mill on the island of Mindanao, up in the mountains. Life was great. Then one day the Japanese bombed the Philippines.

Fred led the Morro tribesman in guerrilla warfare against the Japs. The Morros would capture the Japs and take them up into the mountains, and kill them very slowly. The torture the Morros used is another story. Fred and his wife had a son who was a scout for the American army. In the end, the son became an American citizen, and the last I heard of him, he had retired from the U. S. Army as a full Colonel, living in Northern California.

After World War II, Fred and his wife moved to Calcutta, India. Fred made a good living in the world of smuggling. From India he moved to Africa. After a very long walk across Africa, he ended up in Rio de Janeiro, Brazil. From Rio de Janeiro he moved to Guayaquil, Ecuador. By this time he could speak seventeen languages, and he managed a hotel in Guayaquil. This is where I met Fred David and his Russian wife. Fred was known as a "China

Coaster," or a man whose word is beyond reproach.

I went into the bank of Tamaco, in Guayaquil one time, for some business transaction. I would need a reference, so I told the banker to call Fred David at the hotel. The bank called Fred and he told them to give me any amount of money I asked for. The banker was extremely nice to me. Fred's word was beyond reproach. This is the man I was talking to, and this is the man I was going to take to the United States.

We talked long into the night, and they stayed on board that night. Fruit was coming aboard at the rate of about four hundred stems an hour, so the time consumed was about forty-five hours. We loaded all the next day and well into the night. About 2200 the loading ports were secured, the pilot was aboard and we began hoisting the anchor. We turned the ship around to head down the river and the pilot said, "You know the way out. Goodbye and have a nice trip. " With that, the pilot got in his launch and was gone. We were still off of Puerto Bolivar.

As we were pilot house control, I pushed the controls to slow ahead, and looked for the light on the sea buoy. Fred and Nada were in the pilot house talking a mile a minute, and I was trying to find my way down the river. The river is narrow, and there is a mud bank on the starboard side. I could see the light on the sea buoy, just off the starboard bow, and knew we were all right. All I wanted to do was to get into deep water and relax.

In the faint light of the pilot house, Nada was asking me questions about the ship. I was trying to answer her and watch that light on the starboard bow, when Ortega ran in.

Ortega handled all of the smuggling for the crew. As he ran into the pilot house, he yelled that we were going too fast, the canoes couldn't keep up with the ship. I stopped the propulsion motor, gave the ship a little left rudder, and tried to back down a little. I didn't want to put the ship full astern because we would swing to starboard, and into the mud bank. We might pull the canoes into the stern of the ship and have a lot of trouble. Fred ran out on the wing of the bridge, looked astern and then yelled at me

146

out on the wing of the bridge, looked astern and then yelled at me to go ahead. The canoes would never catch us.

I put the ship to half speed, and watched the little white light off of the starboard bow. Ortega came back in and said that he couldn't unload the cigarettes, as we were going too fast. Everyone was talking at once, so I calmly asked if they would all close their mouths for a minute. Turning to Ortega, I told him that no one had told me anything about dropping off the cigarettes. We had not gone dockside in Panama, and no cargo had come aboard, so what was he smuggling?

We cleared Jambeli Point and I changed course to west by south, and at full speed we ran for the open ocean. Rounding Santa Clara Island on our starboard hand, we headed north for Panama. I brought out a bottle of Scotch whiskey, and after pouring a round of drinks, I sat down in my big chair. It was well after midnight and I was dead tired. The ship was on auto-pilot and two seamen were on watch. I finished my drink, said goodnight to Fred and Nada, and went down to my room. Laying down on my bunk, I was immediately in the arms of Morpheus.

We traveled north across the Gulf of Panama and arrived at the Panama Canal. The Canal Zone is an area five miles on each side of the center of the canal, making it ten miles wide, that was relinquished to the United States in perpetuity. Perpetuity means the quality or condition of being perpetual, or forever.

Fred and Nada were overjoyed to be able to view the canal from the standpoint of a small ship in transit, as it locked up and traveled through the cut, and then across the lake. We locked down the three locks that took us down eighty-three feet, and with the pilot going ashore in his launch, we proceeded into the Caribbean Sea.

We had good weather, with an easterly sea and whitecaps. The ship was heavy with cargo, so the waves frequently broke over the lower deck. This is good weather in the Caribbean. When the weather is dead calm, beware. There's probably a hurricane making up or blowing somewhere.

Most of our nine days running northbound were spent up on the bridge. Although we were a small vessel, John and I had two large chairs installed on the bridge. As we spent most of our waking time there, why not be in comfort? Fred and Nada would sit in the chairs, and I would sit on the chart table. Fred and I spent many hours talking about his life in China, the war in the Philippines, and his life in India. He didn't say much about the long walk across Africa, or the time spent in Brazil. We talked about his life in Ecuador, and how he became the president of the hotel owners' association. Then we arrived in Galveston, Texas.

With the pilot on board and Galveston Island on our port hand, we proceed up the ship channel. We turned to the left and docked at pier 22, Galveston Island, Texas. The quarantine doctor came aboard and we passed through quarantine. Then the Customs and Immigration officers came on board. Customs was no problem, just the normal cargo and paperwork. Now came the Immigration officers.

The crew was out on deck opening the loading ports, and an oil barge was coming alongside, as Fred and Nada sat down at the large galley table. I sat down beside Fred, and looked at the three Customs officers on the other side of the table. I could see the battle lines between the United States Government and Fred David were being formed. The papers from the American Embassy in Ecuador were spread out on the table.

The Customs officers scrutinized each individual paper. They held the papers to the light and looked for watermarks. Then the questioning started. For the next hour, Fred told them his life story. When he was finished, one of the Customs officers looked at Fred and said, "There never was a French-American Tobacco Company in Shanghai. It was the British-American Tobacco Company. "

Fred looked him in the eye and said, "I am sorry, but you are wrong! It was the French-American Tobacco Company. "

There was silence about the decks. I could hear the men yelling out on the dock, then one of the Customs officers asked a very simple question. "Mister David, where did you learn to speak English?"

That simple question opened a huge door. A Russian spy would have all of his papers in order, and be able to speak many languages including excellent English. Nada began to cry. I got up from the table and took Nada to the ship's office. I reassured Nada that everything would be all right, then returned to the battle with the Immigration at the table. .

While I was in the office with Nada, one of the Customs officers had gone ashore. This officer went to a telephone on the dock, and called the Immigration office in Washington, D. C. As I walked into the galley, this officer returned. He looked at Fred and said, "Mister David, I apologize, You are right. It was the French-American Tobacco Company in Shanghai in 1933. We are proud to have you in the United States. You are the type of person we wish to have here in our country. "

The entire story was true. After more than an hour of interrogation, the three Customs officers shook hands with Fred, and we all had a cup of coffee. Fred David had entered the United States and had a home. Fred now had a place to be buried when he died. Nada wiped the tears away, and was bubbling over with joy. With his arm around Nada, Fred was smiling from ear to ear.

Fred and Nada moved to Florida, where her daughter and son-in-law lived. I quit going to sea and returned to my wife and family in San Diego. Now you know how the "China Coaster" came to America. And now, as I write this short story, Fred is in that great world beyond.

Cut Off His Ears.

It all started on a Saturday afternoon, when we were moored at the "B" Street pier in San Diego, California. Our cargo of bananas was almost unloaded, and the Captain had headed up to San Pedro, where he lived. The Captain, John Radine, had told me that he was thinking of hiring another man. John said we needed a second mate, to just work the crew. He didn't have to know any navigation, just be able to stand a watch, and run the crew. I concurred with John. It would make my job easier. I was second in command, and had to work thirty hours a day to keep up. There just wasn't enough time.

I leaned on the rail of the Atlantic Reefer, and watched this slightly built man saunter down the dock. With his hands in his pockets, he stopped and watched the operation. The long-shore-men were unloading two cargo holds, and we were almost finished.

This twenty-five-year-old man ducked under the conveyors that were unloading the fruit, and came to a halt in front of me. He said hello, and I returned the greeting. Then we talked about the fruit. He asked where it came from, and I told him Mexico. He told me he was a seaman from Canada, and out of a job. He wanted to know if he could have a sandwich and cup of coffee. He looked like he needed some food, so I asked him to come aboard. The sandwich and coffee were no problem, and besides, he might be just the one we needed for a second mate. He walked up the gangplank.

I lead him into the galley, and got out the bread, butter, meat and two cups. I told him to make his own sandwich, as I poured two cups of coffee. He made a big sandwich, with lots of meat, and by the way he ate it, he was extremely hungry. He drank his coffee black. I liked that. He just drank the coffee, as is.

As we sat there, I asked him his name and where he was from. His name was Joseph Amie Savoy. He sailed on small freighters, mostly coastwise. Joe was half French and half something else.

He sounded like a good seaman, and he was surely hungry. He finished the large, beef sandwich, and asked if he could have another. I told him, "Certainly, eat all you want. "

Joe and I walked back out on deck and watched the unloading. We both had a cup of coffee in hand, and I sounded him out with small talk. After a half hour, I had a very good idea of what kind of man he was. Joe was an American Citizen, although he was born in Canada. He had American seaman's papers and had been sailing on tug boats, mostly coast wise. He didn't speak much Spanish, but then we could live with that. I told Joe, he would have to speak with the Captain about employment. Meanwhile, he could eat on the ship, but to keep his hotel room ashore.

Joe returned for dinner that night. After dinner I broke out a bottle and we sat on deck with a cold drink. We looked at the lights of San Diego, and made a little small talk. As he departed, I asked him back for Sunday breakfast. With nothing else to do, I stretched out in my bunk and started reading a book.

Sunday morning I was up bright and early. After saying good morning to the cook, I poured a cup of coffee and stepped out on deck. There was Joe, sitting on an old box on the pier. I asked him aboard for breakfast, and he was delighted. For a skinny man, he ate like a horse.

Monday, about noon, Capt. John came back from San Pedro. Joe was waiting for him, and they had a short talk. John came over to me, and asked what I thought of him. I told John that if we didn't like him, we could let him go, next time we were in San Diego. John hired Joe, and that afternoon, Joe brought his gear aboard. I had plenty of room in my quarters, and an extra bunk. We decided Joe would bunk with me.

We took on bunkers and water on Monday. About sundown, we cleared San Diego bound for Manzinillo, Mexico. We ran a few days down the cost of Baja, California, then we cut across the Gulf, and a few more hours brought us to Manzinillo. Usually we would spend two or three days loading bananas and limes, then back up to San Diego.

We made this Manzinillo run for about six months. Then our boss, Anton Martinolich came aboard one afternoon. We all sat in the galley and drank coffee, while Tony gave us this long tirade about losing money. In the end, he told us he had chartered the Atlantic Reefer with the West Indies' Fruit Company, in Miami, Florida. We had worked for them before, so we knew that we were back on the run to Ecuador and Columbia. I asked Joe if he had ever worked that area, and he said no.

We took the Reefer down to Martinolich Shipyard, and cleaned her up. The engineers checked over the engines, and picked up all the spare parts they could. Up on the deck we painted and checked all rigging. Then Joe and I walked through the shipyard, and picked up anything we thought we would need. Our boss, Anton Martinolich, owned the Shipyard and the Atlantic Reefer, so we felt that anything in the yard we could have for the Reefer.

The day came when we let go the lines, blew the whistle, and cleared San Diego. Our next stop would be Talara, Peru. We took on bunkers at Talara, and then ran up to Guayaquil, Ecuador. John and I went ashore in Guayaquil, and it was like an old home week. We had hauled fruit out of there for several years, but not this last year. We took Joe with us and introduced him to all of our friends. Next day we started loading fruit, and in another day we were headed up the cost to Panama.

We were now on the run from Miami or Galveston, Texas, down through the Panama Canal and on to Ecuador. We would load fruit somewhere in Ecuador, and haul it back to the States, via Panama Canal. We had made this run before, so nothing was new.

Joe had never worked this area, and it was all new to him. We introduced him to people in various sea ports, and he became well acquainted. Joe had a great personality, and he was a likable person. The months rolled by, and we made trip after trip. Sometimes we went to Puerto Bolivar, Ecuador, and sometimes we were in Guayaquil. Now and then we would haul a load of fruit out of Esmeraldas. The Esmeraldas fruit was poor quality.

The Atlantic Reefer was chartered to the West Indies Fruit Company, of Miami, Florida. In our contract with the fruit company, there was a clause that stipulated we must maintain a fifteen-knot average between ports. The Government published a book, called H. O. 117. This book is a table of the distance from one port to another, all over the world. A bookkeeper in the office would have one of these books. They look at the distance between ports, divide by fifteen, and have the number of hours of transit.

The Reefer had a hard time making fifteen knots. As all courses are normally set for five miles off of the land, I started setting courses closer to shore. At last, Capt. John told me to dive down and look at the propeller. As the propeller gathers barnacles, so the ship will slow down. While we were moored at pier two in Miami, I put on a face mask and dove down to the propeller. It was covered with barnacles.

I made my report to John. John, in turn, called Anton Martinolich. When John came back to the ship, he told us that we would be in San Diego within two or three months. I set courses closer to land, and ran in closer to various reefs.

At last came the day when we cleared Miami, and had orders to pick up a load of fruit in Ecuador. We loaded fruit in Guayaquil, and with a last drink at the Majestic Hotel, we were bound for San Diego, California.

Our course to San Diego took us east of the Galapagos Islands. I wanted to go through the Islands, and pick up some good eating fish from some of my friends there. John wouldn't hear of it.

For the past two years we had worked the banana run from Ecuador to the States. Like all ships that pursue this trade, the crew had their own little business. When we went southbound, we would pick up cigarettes, whiskey, and women's under clothing. At various times we carried cases of apples, baby food and outboard motors. In fact, we carried a wide variety of items to be

153

smuggled into the country. Seamen make more money smuggling than they do in wages.

Every man in the crew was in the smuggling business, except Joe. For some unknown reason, Joe would not be involved in this business. I knew that something was wrong, the first time I spoke to Joe about the smuggling business. Each one of us had cash money to purchase various items, to sell on our next trip south. Now we were heading to San Diego, so all of our money was put away. There is never any business going into the United States. All of the items we took south, could be purchased in the United States.

We ran into San Diego and unloaded the fruit. When we were finished with our cargo, we took the Reefer to Martinolich Shipyard. The ship was put in dry dock, and all of the ship's power was shut down. Lines were run aboard for electric power and the crew lived aboard. Men from the shipyard swarmed over the Reefer. There were men working in the engine room, and men cleaning outside. We would be in dry dock for a long week.

The Chief Engineer and I decided to go hunting in northern California. We knew some people in Preather, California, and they said we could hunt up there.

At that time, I had about five or six thousand dollars that were used to purchase commodities for the run to Ecuador. This money was locked in a metal sea chest, and under my bunk. Joe had a sea chest under his bunk, also. We both had keys to the door, so we could lock our room when in port. Out at sea, who would steal?

I took about a thousand dollars, my . 270 deer rifle, and we headed north. The hunt was great. The catching was a little poor. We climbed up on ledges, behind this little town, and watched goats as they grazed. There was a little rain, and a lot of clouds. I had one shot at a goat, and missed. The Chief shot one old goat, as he was eating some berries from a tree. We left the goat with the people we knew, and headed back to San Diego.

I climbed up on the dry dock, and was met by half of the crew.

Each one was trying to tell me something in Spanish. I finely got them to stop talking, and singled out one man to explain the problem. Very slowly the story unraveled. I was the one that had a problem, not them.

The crew told me that Joe had all new clothes. He had a beautiful tweed suit, with an overcoat to match. I was told that he was drinking in a bar called the Buccaneero, in National City. Joe had a string of girls following him. That could mean only one thing. Joe had a lot of money. He never took part in our little smuggling business. Where did Joe get the money? He stole it either from ashore, or from the ship, and I had a good idea. I asked where Joe was, and I was told that he was ashore.

I went to my room, unlocked the door, and slowly pulled my sea chest out from under my bunk. The lock had been cut by a big pair of bolt cutters. We had bolt cutters in the engine room. I opened the chest and looked inside. My money was gone. I couldn't believe it. I took everything out of the chest, and placed it on my bunk. There was no question about it. I had been robbed, and Joe was the culprit.

John was in San Pedro, so I called the chief engineer. We sat at the galley table, thinking what to do. Reluctantly I called the San Diego Police Department. I explained what had happened, and was told to wait on the ship. In about an hour, two detectives arrive on the Reefer. Once again I went over every detail, and showed them my sea chest. I did not know exactly how much money I had in the chest, but it was about four thousand dollars.

The detectives departed, and I was left to ponder this new problem in my life. The next morning I received a phone call from one of the detectives. They had Joe locked up in jail. They wanted me to identify him, to be sure it was the right man.

I drove over to the jail, in San Diego, and went in. After identifying myself, we walked back into the holding cells. There was Joe, huddled in a corner, and trying to sober up. I don't deal with jails, drunks and street bums. It was a surprise to see how far down the ladder of life that Joe had fallen. Every door in his life had suddenly closed. He was now a nothing, crawling in a corner of the San Diego, jail. Joe didn't have a friend. There was no one in his corner for this fight.

I was led out of the holding cells, and to the booking desk. The detective told me I would be notified when Joe would be arraigned. Back on the Reefer, I explained the story of Joe to the crew. I was a little surprised that the crew were more upset about this than I was. There is nothing lower than a sailor that steels from his shipmates. The crew was quite angry with Joe.

Because the Atlantic Reefer was scheduled to head back to the Caribbean, Joe's case was pushed to the front. The next day I received a phone call, telling me to be in court for the arraignment. Cleaning up, and looking my best, I went to the court house.

We stood in front of the judge, and he looked over his glasses first at Joe, and then at me. Joe admitted he could have had four thousand dollars. He only had about three hundred dollars when he was arrested. The judge said he would sentence Joe to twenty years, and I said no, don't do that. If Joe goes to jail, I'll never get any money back. The judge looked at me and gave me a long speech about this type of case. In the end, I asked the judge to let Joe out of jail, and have him pay me back.

Joe was out. I met him walking with a parole officer, just outside the court house building. He was a very sorrowful looking man. I handed Joe twenty dollars. After the four thousand, what was twenty? That is the last time I ever saw Joseph Amie Savoy. Within a few days, we cleared San Diego, and were bound for Guayaquil, Ecuador. I had lost my smuggling money, and now had to start all over.

Joe could not make a living ashore. He only knew the sea. Evidently, Joe talked to his parole officer, and was granted permission to seek employment on a tug boat running from San Diego, to San Pedro. He was picked up for being drunk and disorderly in San Pedro. Then one day Joe dropped out of sight. The police lost track of him. Little Joe had skipped the country.

Meanwhile, the Atlantic Reefer was hauling fruit out of Guayaquil, Ecuador. We made trip after trip. Each trip I would add a few hundred to my little business. At last one afternoon we ran up the Guayas River and anchored off the Malecon. We had a day layover, before we could start loading fruit. The watch was set, and Capt. John and I headed to the Majestic Hotel.

We went into the Majestic, and were greeted by Fred and Nada. Our dinner was served in the dinning room, on the second floor, and Nada sat and talked with us. Fred sat down, after a few minutes, and we all started talking. In short order, Fred told us the latest. Joe was seen in Guayaquil. The information Fred had, was that Joe was trying to join Lopez. Lopez was our contact, and now Joe was trying to cut into the business.

John and I finished dinner, chatted with Fred and Nada, then returned to the Reefer. We climbed up on the deck, and were met by some of the crew. The crew told us the same thing. Joe was seen in Guayaquil. These Indians are all related, and somewhere, Joe had crossed Lopez. One thing about smuggling, you are honest, or you are dead. The word was out to get Joe. John and I went into the office, and tried to think what to do.

That night, there were only a few men on the ship, just enough to stand the watch. We were all up bright and early. About noon, the first load of fruit came along side. It was tied off, the loading ramps were put in place, and the fruit started aboard. I gave the banana grader his usual bottle of whiskey and carton of cigarettes. For good luck, I gave him my wrist watch. The company purchased the watches by the dozen, and we handed them out just as fast. These little gratuities make life easier in these ports.

Several hours after dinner, one of the crew came up to me and said, "John wants to see you, he's in the office. " I went below, and entered the office. John told me to sit down, he had something he wanted to show me. I sat down in a chair, and John reached over to the desk. He withdrew a paper bag, just a small, plain paper bag. Handing it to me, he said, "Look in there. " I took the bag and looked in.

At first I didn't understand what was in the bag. It looked like two pieces of beef jerky, only not so dried up. I looked at John and said, "What is it?" Without changing the expression on his face he said, "They are ears, and the crew says they're Joe's!"

I looked in the paper bag again. They did look like ears. I couldn't believe it. There was a pair of ears in that bag. I handed the bag back to John, and said, "I don't believe it. " We sat there in silence, for what seemed like an eternity. At last John said, "Well, they're someone's ears, and whoever it was, is dead now. I'll talk to Fred tomorrow, before we leave. " With that, I went out, to take a turn around the deck.

It was just daylight, when I sat down to breakfast. John came in about the same time. We talked about the fruit for a few minutes, then he went ashore. I finished breakfast and went out on deck. The endless chain of men carrying bananas up the wooden gangplank had worked all night. Utilizing both loading doors, we could load a thousand stems an hour. The big hold up, was ashore. Some trips we would wait for several hours, while the lighters were being loaded. This trip the fruit was coming in steady.

Captain John was back aboard by noon, and we just finished loading the last stem of bananas. The ship came to life, as the engineer started the big main generators. I checked the loading ports. They were secure. John and the pilot were on the bridge, so I started heaving in the anchor. As the anchor cleared the water, John turned the Reefer around, and we started down the Guayas River. Twenty-nine miles down the river, the pilot went ashore. We now headed for the open ocean.

As we ran along the shore of Puna Island, I walked around the ship. Everything was secure, and we were ready for sea. Going up to the bridge, I found John seated in his big chair. I sat down in mine, and put my feet up on the engine room telegraph stand. A seaman went below and brought back coffee for all of us. We were clear of land, and all of its troubles, so now it was time to talk.

As we rolled north bound, in a gentle swell, we talked of Joe and the ears. There was no doubt, there were human ears in that sack. Neither John nor I thought they belonged to Joe.

When John was ashore, he had spent some time talking with Fred. The story was out, that Lopez gave Joe a lot of money to pay for a load of contraband. Joe had a few drinks, flashed the money around the bar, and was last seen entering a taxi. The word got back to Lopez, in a matter of minutes. Within an hour, a contract was out on Joe. This is the last we ever heard of Joseph Amie Savoy.

John and I agreed that those were not Joe's ears. I have no idea whose they are, probably some old bush Indian. You can purchase a shrunken head for forty American dollars. So, ears would be easy to come by.

John brought the sack out of his room, and threw it in the ocean. The last I saw of the sack, with the ears, it was bobbing merrily in the wake of the Atlantic Reefer. As the sun went down, John and I sat in our chairs on the bridge, each of us engrossed in our own thoughts of Little Joe.